APR 2

JF
Collier, Kristi.
Throwing stones

THROWING STONES

KRISTI COLLIER

Henry Holt and Company
New York

Henry Holt and Company, LLC
Publishers since 1866
175 Fifth Avenue
New York, New York 10010
www.henryholtchildrensbooks.com

Henry Holt® is a registered trademark of Henry Holt and Company, LLC.
Copyright © 2006 by Kristi Collier
All rights reserved.
Distributed in Canada by H. B. Fenn and Company Ltd.

Library of Congress Cataloging-in-Publication Data
Collier, Kristi.
Throwing stones / Kristi Collier.—1st ed.
p.   cm.
Summary: In 1923, in Pierre, Indiana, fourteen-year-old Andy realizes a
dream when he makes the high school basketball team, but when an accident
keeps him from playing, he ventures into journalism and begins to under-
stand the meaning of sportsmanship.
ISBN-13: 978-0-8050-7614-1
ISBN-10: 0-8050-7614-X
[1. High schools—Fiction.   2. Schools—Fiction.   3. Basketball—Fiction.
4. Journalism—Fiction.   5. Sportsmanship—Fiction.   6 Coming of age—
Fiction.   7. Indiana—History—20th century—Fiction.]   I. Title.
PZ7.C6793Th 2006   [Fic]—dc22   2006000724

First edition—2006
Printed in the United States of America on acid-free paper ∞
1   3   5   7   9   10   8   6   4   2

The excerpt on page 10 is from the poem "Marcus Bozzaris"
by Fitz-Greene Halleck (1790–1867).

Especially for Dad

Chapter One

"You want to see a naked girl?"

"What?" I spun my head around so fast the muscle in my neck popped, sending shards of pain rocketing down my shooting arm. My best friend, Ham, smirked and sat against a boulder that flanked the edge of the abandoned quarry. He kicked his feet out in front of him and propped one bare foot on top of the other.

"I said . . ." Ham paused, letting his words linger. He looked like he hadn't a care in the world, but he was sucking the life out of a blade of alfalfa grass. "Do you want to see a—"

"I heard you," I said quickly. A picture of Ham's younger sister, AnnaLise, popped into my mind. I wondered if she was the naked girl Ham was talking about. In his family, with five sisters running around, it was certainly a possibility. The thought made my stomach feel funny. I wiped the palms of my hands on my pants.

"Aw, you're full of baloney," I said. I rolled my shoulders and tried to ease out the cramp. The pain inched its way from one side of my neck to the other.

"Am not. I'm dead shooting serious." Ham spat the alfalfa grass to the ground, flipped to his feet, and crouched in front of me. I thought that if Ham could channel his maniac energy, he'd be a great guard for the basketball team. But Ham didn't care about things that had rules and organization.

"Naked girls. Hundreds of 'em. Well, at least a couple. And they take *all* their clothes off." Ham's voice rose to a squeak. He was standing now and pacing. I stood up. I was taller than Ham and bigger, but my energy was more contained. Deliberate, Ham would say. Wary.

Ham leaned in close and whispered, "They're at the carnival. In a tent. A naked girl tent."

I stepped back and stared at him. Part of me was relieved he wasn't talking about AnnaLise. But the other part . . . I shook my head. "The carnival? You're crazy. We can't go to the carnival."

Every year a group of roustabouts drifted into town with their tents and their freaks and their lures of easy prizes. They set up in a field north of town and took money from the scabblers coming from the quarries and the car blockers coming from the railroad. It sounded wonderful, but I was never allowed to go. Neither was Ham. I reminded him of that fact again. Ham only smiled.

"It's not like we're going to ask permission, Andy." Ham's eyes crinkled in that funny way he had when plotting mischief. "We'll sneak out, under cover of darkness."

His voice rose dramatically, then he crouched low and took two steps forward. "We'll cut through the Oberstrong's pastures and come at the carnival from the back side. If my sources serve me well, the naked girls are located at the far right corner. We can peek under the tent, see the naked girls, and then bolt for home before anyone even notices that we're gone." He grinned.

"Boy, oh, boy, Ham. If we get caught . . ." I let the awful idea hang in the air for a moment. "My parents would kill me. Yours, too."

Ham shook his head. The look of deviousness on his face softened. "The Judge won't do anything."

As strange as it sounded, I had to admit that Ham was right. Judge Mortimer was reputed to be the toughest judge in the county. Everybody knew it, from the stonecutters to the farmers to Willard Nevil, the town drunk. But no matter what kind of trouble Ham got himself into, the Judge never punished him. The Judge would stand, stern and un-moving, the anger and disappointment carved into his face. Sometimes he'd make Ham pay what he called restitution, but when it came right down to it, he never actually sen-tenced Ham to any kind of punishment. I often wondered if Ham got into trouble just to see if he could get a reac-tion out of his father. I wished my parents would let me get away with half the stuff the Judge let Ham get away with.

Then Ham shook his head and the grin returned. "Felix, on the other hand, would have a fit." The idea seemed to strike Ham as funny. Felix was Ham's uncle, the Judge's brother. He was also the county sheriff, but we joked that he should have been born a preacher. He could talk a jaybird quiet. And boy did he rattle on about the Catholics brewing their illegal beer and the flappers with their short skirts. Most folks, my brother George included, took Sheriff Mortimer's words as gospel. But Ham, being Ham, thought his uncle was full of hot air.

"I don't know, Ham," I said.

Ham must have taken my uncertainty as a yes. "I'll meet you behind your barn tonight at ten o'clock."

I shook my head. "I can't. Tonight is Pete's birthday."

Ham's face clouded. "Oh. Sorry. I forgot." Then he brightened. "Thursday, then. Same time."

"But . . ." I had to find some way out of this. "Won't your parents still be awake?" Everyone in my family woke with the sun to milk the cows, so we fell asleep early. But Ham's family sometimes stayed awake until midnight.

"Eleven o'clock, then. Bye!" Ham grinned and raced toward town.

I picked up the stone I'd been carving and with my finger traced the lines I'd etched. It looked pretty good, I thought, almost like a real basketball. I stuck the carving in my pocket. I trudged past the boulders that littered the ground around the abandoned quarry, toward the house, the last place I wanted to be. Tonight was Pete's birthday. Ham had forgotten. I sighed. I could never forget. Some days I thought I was stuck at age eight, the day I discovered that Pete had run off to war. Or maybe age nine, the day I learned that he was never coming back.

Chapter Two

We always ate the same thing, every August 14, Pete's favorite meal—roasted chicken in its own gravy, sweet corn drowning in butter, and red tomatoes off the vine. For dessert—triple berry pie and a dollop of whipped cream. Pete was the same age as the year; he would have been twenty-three today. It had been six years since he ran off to war, five years since he died. If anybody thought it strange that the only time we ever mentioned him was on his birthday, no one ever said so.

After supper, we cleared the plates to the side. Dad took down the velvet box and slowly opened it to display Pete's medals. The box was black, with an inner lining of burgundy satin that reminded me of pooled blood. The medals glistened dully in the soft glow of the oil lamp.

The telegram lined the top of the box, wedged into place. That awful telegram—frayed now at the edges and yellow with age. Father read the telegram, had for the last five years. As many times as I'd heard it, I still couldn't believe it was true. There had to be some mistake. Pete wouldn't go and die, not like that.

The day we got that telegram, November 11, 1918, the newspaper ran an extra edition. The armistice had been signed and the Kaiser had surrendered. The war was over! Schools let out early and businesses closed so everyone could celebrate. There was a parade that stretched clear down Main Street. Car horns tooted, horses whinnied, and Ham and I tore up Mrs. Pickens's newspapers to make confetti.

We were still celebrating when Mr. McAllistair from the railroad office walked toward Dad with the telegram in his hand; the telegram saying that Pete had died. Not from an enemy bullet, but from influenza. Seemed to me God had reached down from heaven as if to shake our hands, but then surprised us with a punch in the gut.

I clutched the letter in my hands. It was barely readable now, crumpled and faded, but I knew what it said. It was from Pete, written to me the night he left for the war, and it said he would come to cheer for me when I led the team to the state basketball tournament. He promised. So there had to be a mistake. The telegram couldn't be true. Even after all these years.

The weight of Pete's basketball pressed against my legs. It was my basketball now, and I kept the brown leather clean and good as new. Ready and waiting. The Pierre Carvers, that's what we called our team. After Pete led the team to back-to-back sectional championships two years in a row, nearly defeating Lafayette and Lebanon at the state tournament, the school board voted to build a new gym. Pete's gym, I called it.

Dad finished reading the telegram, and then George read a scripture verse, I Corinthians 15:55. He always recited it the same way, the words slow and clear, his mouth widely forming each individual letter. Sort of like my grammar school teacher used to talk. I used to wonder if she was a bit stupid. Maybe she just thought we were. George was only three years older than me, but he talked to me the same way that teacher had. This year I'd show him, I thought as I touched the basketball. This year I'd be the team's leading scorer. I started to smile at the thought of George, a senior, sitting on the bench while I played. Then I remembered that I was supposed to be sad, so I tried to think of something else.

"I come to the garden alone," Mother sang. Her voice warbled in the quiet room. Her eyes took on a luminous, faraway glow when she sang. Mother had changed when Pete went off to war. She stopped playing bridge with the other ladies in town and she started doing good works. Maybe she thought if she did enough good deeds then God would see fit to send Pete home. It hadn't worked. Even though Pete was gone and the work made her tired, Mother kept on knitting blankets and mending clothes.

"Thank you, Beatrice," Dad said when the last notes of Mother's song faded into silence. He cleared his throat and began to speak.

"But to the hero, when his sword
   Has won the battle for the free,
   Thy voice sounds like a prophet's word
   And in its hollow tones are heard
   The thanks of millions yet to be."

Dad had changed when Pete left, too. Dad had always been strong. He had thick hands and massive shoulders and legs the size of tree trunks. But when Pete died he cracked, somehow, like a rock pulled from the quarry so late in the season that it fissured and split from an early freeze. All the laughter and strength seeped out of him through those cracks.

I took a deep breath. Maybe this year I could fill the Pete-sized hole that had nearly swallowed our family when he died. Maybe I could make my dad laugh again. Maybe I could make my mother want to talk and gossip with the other ladies in town. Maybe, finally, I could start to feel like I really meant something to our family. George was just like mother, prim and well-mannered, so there was no doubt that my parents loved him. Pete, the bravest, strongest, smartest person I knew, had been just like Dad. I was the one who always felt out of place, the same way the littered boulders of the abandoned quarry looked out of place on our otherwise productive farm. But if I could take the bas-ketball team to state, then maybe I could belong, too.

I didn't say anything, I never had. I rubbed the stitching on the ball and waited for it to be over. I couldn't get a pic-ture of Pete by looking at a medal, or by listening to a song. It was only when I held a basketball in my hands that I remembered him.

Mother closed the box, placed it back on the shelf, and went to tidy the kitchen. Father retired to the living room to study the *Farmer's Almanac* by the dim light of the lamp. George went to the room we shared. I walked outside with a coal oil lantern and my basketball, to the familiar comfort of the barn wall with the basketball hoop. Five years. Next year would be six and we'd do it all again.

But next year would be different, I thought as I watched the ball rattle through the wrought iron hoop. Next year my parents would be proud of me. And next year, maybe, just maybe, our family could be happy again.

Chapter Three

"Andrew!" Two days later, on Thursday morning, Dad's voice broke into my concentration as I sighted the basket from twenty feet away.

I stood straight and tried to hide the basketball behind my back. "Yes, sir?"

"Your mother said water is leaking across the kitchen floor." He looked me over. "Did you empty the ice pan?"

"Um . . ." I wished I was as quick-witted as Ham and could think of a smart answer. But then, Ham didn't have chores. "No, sir, not yet. I was just going to . . ."

"Do it now! Your mother has enough to do without having to mop the floor because you were irresponsible." Dad's face looked worn. I wondered if he had gotten any sleep before waking up at four to milk the cows. "Just because the wheat's been threshed doesn't mean we don't have a lot of work to do to keep this farm afloat. There's still the last cut of hay to bale and the corn to shock and shuck and the butchering—"

"Yes, sir," I said.

I tucked my basketball under my arm and walked toward the house. The large block of ice that kept the icebox cool melted quickly on hot days and filled the ice pan. It was my job to empty it into the animals' watering trough.

George was leaving the kitchen as I walked toward it. "I finished filling the wood box," he said. "You forgot to do that, too." George crossed his arms over his chest. "Lazy hands are the Devil's playground."

"Why don't you sew yourself a sampler," I said between clenched teeth.

"There's no need to be rude," George said. "It's time you learned some responsibility. Instead of spending all your time playing." He leaned forward and before I could blink he knocked the basketball out from underneath my arm. He dribbled it and then held it between his hands.

"Give that back!" I hollered. I lunged at him, but he turned away.

"When you're finished with your chores, then you can have it back," he said. He held the basketball high, just out of reach. He was less than an inch taller than I was, but his arms were longer. I jumped and tried to knock the ball out of his hands, but he swiveled out of reach.

I stood, defeated, and let my arms hang down at my sides. "You're right," I said. "Maybe I should be more like you, a responsible, well-mannered, flat tire." George cocked his head, but I didn't give him a chance to respond. "Of course, maybe that's why Norma Campbell wouldn't let you walk her home after the Sunday school picnic last week."

George scowled. "Why you little . . ."

I turned quickly and plowed into him, knocking the basketball loose. It bounced toward the house. I raced after it, but George was right behind me, grabbing at my overalls.

I stopped and twisted, letting George's anger throw him off balance. Then I grabbed his right arm, turned, and pulled. George lost his footing and landed on his stomach. I straddled his back, still holding on to his arm. He twisted and flailed, but I had him pinned. Score one for me. It was Pete who had taught me that move. Good way to take down someone bigger and stronger.

"Say uncle."

"You let me go right now or I'll toss you headfirst into the abandoned quarry and leave you there until the buzzards pick you clean."

I grinned. It seemed Mr. George Soaring wasn't so well mannered and responsible after all. "Say uncle."

George squirmed. "You are a dim-witted, overgrown beast."

"Say it. Uncle, uncle, uncle."

"You want me to say uncle? Fine, I'll say it. Uncle! You happy? Now get off, you stupid little boy!"

The little boy comment stung, but I climbed off and helped him to his feet. He swatted my hands away and brushed off his trousers. Then he shook his head. "When are you going to grow up?"

"Aw, come on. You started it." I loped toward the house and grabbed my basketball. I felt better with it tucked under my arm. "After I empty the ice pan, you want to shoot some baskets?"

George closed his eyes slowly and then opened them again, as if he didn't like what he saw. "I have more important things to do than play with you," he said evenly.

"You're just afraid I'm gonna whoop you and take your starting spot on the team." I smirked. "But you can cheer from the bench when we win state."

George flinched. The one area of his life in which he wasn't entirely perfect was basketball. Even though he played consistently by the rules, he had yet to lead the team to a winning season. "Freshmen don't play varsity ball. Coach Crowley won't even let you on the floor. It's you who's going to be cheering from the bench. Now move. I'm going to help Dad mend the cultivator."

George walked away, his back ramrod straight. I stared after him. I'd show him, I thought. I'd show everyone.

"Andrew!" Mother's voice floated through the open window. I turned and trudged into the kitchen.

Mother sat at the table, knitting fringe onto a stack of small, quilted blankets. Baby blankets, probably for an orphanage somewhere.

A pot of stew bubbled on top of the woodstove. I peeked into the pot and took a deep breath of the savory smell.

"Please check the flame," Mother said.

"Yes, ma'am." I used a rag to open the wood box on the stove. A wave of heat from glowing red embers billowed out. I wiped my forehead with my sleeve, and then tossed a couple of corncobs and a piece of kindling into the flames. The stove used a massive amount of fuel that George and I were supposed to replenish, even in August when the house was already sweltering.

I pulled the ice pan from underneath the icebox and carried it outside. Water splashed my overalls. Before I poured the water into the animal trough, I cooled my face.

"It's empty," I said after I returned the ice pan. I grabbed a rag and mopped up the spills.

"Thank you," Mother said. Her knitting needles clacked in a soothing rhythm. A sheen of sweat covered her forehead, but she didn't slow. Clack, clackety-clack, clack, clack.

I turned to go back outside when Mother said, "Ham telephoned earlier."

"He did?" I looked at the telephone with a sinking feeling. Oh, no. The carnival. I had forgotten. "What did he say?"

"Nothing worth telephoning about. Just that he would see you later." Mother's needles paused for a moment as she looked at me. "Is he up to something?"

"Ham?" I said, feeling desperate. "No. He's not. Nothing."

Mother's knitting needles resumed. "I don't know what his mother is thinking, letting him use the telephone for no purpose other than chatting. Such extravagance."

"May I call him back?" I asked, staring at the large box on the wall. Several years earlier Dad and a couple of neighbor men put up poles and lines to connect the surrounding farms with the Pierre exchange. But even though we had a telephone, we didn't use it very often.

Mother's needles stopped with a resounding CLACK. "Certainly not," she said. "The telephone is not a toy." She stood and straightened her work. "I need you to pick the ripe vegetables. I am going to can this afternoon."

I grabbed a bushel basket and sidled out of the house, still staring at the telephone. I didn't have time to walk into town to tell Ham that I couldn't go to the carnival. But Mother was right. It would be an extravagance to telephone. Besides, if I used the telephone, then Mrs. Sniggins, the switchboard operator, and all those other people listening in on the line would know we were up to something. I'd just have to hope that Ham would forget about his plan to sneak into the carnival.

Chapter Four

That night I lay in bed and stared at the darkness of the ceiling. I knew Ham wouldn't forget. What would Pete do? I guessed he'd go. He never was one to back down from a challenge. Anyway, if I didn't meet Ham, he'd probably try to sneak into my room to get me. He'd never find the carnival on his own.

From the other side of the room, George snorted and mumbled in his sleep. Mother said when I was small, Pete and George and I all slept in the same bed. I sure didn't recall sleeping with George, but sometimes, if I closed my eyes and curled into a ball under the quilts, I'd get a sort of remembrance of Pete's presence.

The grandfather clock in the living room chimed. Eleven bongs. I took a deep breath and held it. As I released my breath I swung my legs from under the quilt. I tried to tiptoe across the room, but the wooden floorboards squeaked under my weight. I had grown over the summer, gotten taller and heavier.

George groaned and rolled over. I froze. "Quiet," George muttered. He rolled over again and I started to relax. Then he propped himself up and looked my way. "Where are you going?" he asked sleepily.

"Privy," I said, thinking quickly. "I've really got to go." I shuffled from foot to foot, hoping I looked realistic in the darkness. George, for all his highbrow ways, was nothing but a snitch. Earlier that day he told Dad that I had tackled him, so after dinner Dad made me muck out the cow barn. It didn't seem to matter to anyone that George had started it by taking my basketball. There was nothing worse than having a snitch in your own family.

George lay back down. "Why don't you use the pot?" he mumbled.

"It's a bad one. Gonna stink up the whole room."

"Oh, Andy," George pulled the covers over his head. "Why do you have to be so disgusting?" He rolled back toward the wall.

I smiled, then turned and tiptoed out of the room and down the stairs. I pulled off my nightshirt, which I had worn to bed over my clothes, and stuffed it under the cushions of a chair in the living room. I hoped that George would be sound asleep by the time I got back, and he'd have no idea how long I'd been gone. Otherwise I'd be shoveling manure the rest of my natural-born days.

The screech of what might have been a barn owl pierced the night as I walked toward the barn. One of the cows lowed. I could hear them inside the barn. I turned the corner and saw Ham, silhouetted by the light of the moon, his hands cupped around his mouth. He let out another screech. I clapped a hand on his shoulder and he jumped.

"Whew, Andy! Didn't see you coming. I was beginning to think you chickened out. Did you hear me calling? I'm getting pretty good, aren't I? Come on, let's go. Willard says the carnival starts to wrap up around midnight. Maybe we'll get there just as the naked girls are getting ready for bed." Ham tugged on my arm.

We skirted the abandoned quarry and then walked through pastures fenced for beef cattle and fields of corn ready for harvest. In Pierre, Indiana, there were stone families and there were ordinary families. We used to be a stone family, until ten years ago when our quarry didn't produce limestone like we thought it would. It was supposed to be there, but it wasn't. At least not where we were digging. The quarry broke us. Dad talked about moving to Indianapolis, maybe getting a job with the railroad. It had been Pete's idea to farm the land around the quarry. We'd always kept a vegetable garden, but Pete had been the best at it. He could grow anything.

I let my hand brush against a cornstalk as we passed. In the next month before school started I'd have to spend all of my time in those fields, raking in the last cuttings of hay and shucking bushel upon bushel of corn. I hoped that this year it would be worth it. Since the war ended, the price of corn kept dropping, etching the worry lines deeper into Dad's face. The two-cylinder Whitney tractor he bought three years ago on credit needed a new throttle, and the *Farmer's Almanac* spread fear of an early freeze. Dad worked hard on the farm, and it fed the family, but I knew his heart wasn't in it. He was born and bred a quarrier.

Ham was lucky. He was a town kid, so he didn't have to worry about limestone or corn or anything. He had enough pocket money and free time that he could spend his days at the county jail getting the latest gossip from the deputies and inmates.

"You sure this is the right way?" Ham asked after we had walked about a mile. He turned in a circle, as if he could determine his location in the darkness.

"I'm sure," I said. Ham had no sense of direction. Anna-Lise once joked that he could get lost in his own house. Thinking about AnnaLise made me feel shivery.

We approached the carnival from the west. I could hear the music and the pitches from the barkers long before the tents came into view. The area was lit with oil lamps strung wire-to-wire and post-to-post. Every year one of the town residents sent around a petition trying to ban the carnival because of the risk of fire. But every year the roustabouts came anyway. Nothing bad ever happened unless you counted the black eyes and the jail time imposed by Judge Mortimer on those caught drinking the illegal alcohol.

"Do you think the roustabouts brew their own moonshine or do they sneak it in from Chicago?" I asked.

"Dunno," Ham said. "But the jail's full to the seams with drunks. Uncle Felix is fit to bust. He can't figure out where they're hiding their hooch. He'd confiscate it if he could."

"Was it one of the drunks who told you about the naked girls?" I felt my stomach start to churn.

"Willard Nevil. He said they were beeyooteeful!" Ham tugged on my sleeve. I followed him around the barbed wire that was strung between fence posts. I didn't look forward to climbing that wire.

"That's the one," Ham whispered. He pointed toward a nondescript tent that was lit like all the others. Out in front of it we heard the barker shouting.

"Come one, come all, see the beautiful, voluptuous siren from an ancient land—the graceful and nubile Cleopatra. Only one dollar to see the girl of your dreams."

"What's a siren?" Ham asked. "Is it the same as being naked?"

I opened my mouth to explain, and then sighed. "Yes," I said.

"Well, come on," Ham tugged me closer to the tent, but the call of another barker caught my attention.

"Test your shooting skills. Any challenger who can beat the amazing Bennie and his basketball will win twenty-five dollars. Only two bits to try your luck."

I punched Ham in the arm. "Did you hear that? Twenty-five dollars!"

"Ow." Ham rubbed his shoulder. "Twenty-five dollars? To see Cleopatra? You gotta be kidding! We are *definitely* gonna sneak in." He reached a hand into his pocket. It jingled. "I got about two bucks, most."

"No, not for the girl. For basketball." I drifted toward the basketball goal, which was nothing but a peach basket with a hole in the bottom nailed to a tall post and a couple

22

of rickety boards. Twenty-five dollars. I could buy the parts for the tractor. I could help Dad make a payment on the mortgage. I could even get a new pair of gum-soled canvas basketball shoes. That thought made my heart beat faster. I sure could use a new pair of shoes.

"Basketball!" Ham lunged after me. "We are not here to play basketball! We are here to see a naked girl! Now get your mind back to what's important and follow me."

Ham turned and walked straight into the forbidding form of a carnival worker, unshaven, dressed in dirty overalls and holding a flickering lantern. He was at least a foot taller and one hundred pounds bigger than I was. I tried to swallow the lump that had formed in my throat. Ham let out a nervous giggle.

The roustabout clamped his large hands around our shoulders. I didn't move. I knew that I couldn't, even if I tried. "You boys need some help?" The roustabout's voice was gravelly. His breath smelled sour. I closed my eyes and prayed that he wouldn't kill us.

"We were, uh . . ." My voice cracked. I cleared my throat and tried again. "We were just, uh, going into the carnival."

"The entrance is there." He pointed with his beefy hand. It was so close I could see the dirt encrusted in his fingernails.

"Oh, really? Oh, we didn't know. We didn't see any signs or markers or anything," Ham started babbling. "We were just walking along and I said to my friend here, I said, 'Want to go to the carnival?' and he said, 'Sure,' and I said—"

"You want to see Cleopatra, no?" the roustabout asked. He tilted his head toward the tent.

"Cleopatra? Who's Cleopatra? My buddy here, he heard about the basketball contest, see. He's the best shooter this side of the Mississippi. Never misses. So we just thought we'd check out the basketball, see? But it seems that it's late and you're probably closing up soon, so we'll just be going."

I held my breath and started to tiptoe away. Twenty-five dollars wasn't worth getting killed or beat-up or worse. I had heard stories about travelers that mugged innocent townsfolk, left them for dead, and then disappeared into the next town. I didn't want any part of it. But a hand clapped around my shoulder, making it impossible to move. The pent-up air tightened in my chest.

"Hey, Bennie! We gots a boy says he beat you in the basketball. Come see the basketball boy." The man's voice filled the night. He directed Ham and me away from Cleopatra's tent and toward the center of the carnival, where the peach basket loomed. I glared at Ham. He shrugged helplessly.

A small crowd started to gather around the basket. A dozen pairs of eyes stared at me. I felt my legs grow wobbly. I risked a glance at several of the faces, but didn't see anyone I knew. That was a relief. I tried to guess which of the faces belonged to Bennie, the basketball champion. I imagined he'd be one of the carnival freaks, at least seven feet tall or with arms that hung down to his feet. So when a boy about my age stepped out of the crowd with a ball tucked under his arm, I blinked in surprise.

"You the one wants to beat me in the basketball shooting?" the boy asked. From his build and the shape of his face, I guessed he was related to the carnival worker who had caught us just moments before. He studied me with a skeptical look.

I swallowed and tried to force my head to work. Up, down.

"Two bits." The boy held out a hand.

I froze. I hadn't brought any money. But Ham stepped forward and placed a quarter in the boy's hand. I glared at him. Ham smiled apologetically. The next time I got him alone, I was going to bust him.

"We take turns, same shot. I go first. You match the shot. You miss, you're out."

The feeling started to return to my legs. I knew this game. I had played it with practically every kid in school. "What if *you* miss?" I asked.

The boy grinned and shrugged. "I do not miss."

The crowd backed away, forming a circle around the basket, the boy, and me. The boy dribbled once, stepped back three paces at a right angle to the basket, and shot. The ball launched into the air and fell cleanly through the hole. The audience clapped and hooted. They were all clearly on the boy's side. Bennie took a little bow and stepped away. Someone in the crowd grabbed the basketball and threw it to me.

I caught the ball and stepped to the place where Bennie had stood. I took a deep breath and gazed at the basket. The crowd grew silent, waiting. *What would Pete do?*

Chapter Five

I raised my arms and launched the basketball. For the first time ever, the ball felt bulky and unbalanced in my hands. I wondered frantically if I had lost my shot. At the last second, just before the ball left my fingertips, I gave it an extra shove with my right hand. I stumbled forward with the momentum and landed with a thud on my hands and right knee. Someone in the crowd snickered. I was glad it was dark so that no one could see my face.

The ball banged against the rim of the basket. I heard Ham gasp. The ball wobbled a moment, and then, owing more to luck than to skill, rolled to the side and fell through the hole. It landed on the dirt-packed ground with a dull thump.

"All right!" Ham shouted. Then he quickly clamped his hand over his mouth.

The carnival worker groaned. "Bah," he said. "Lucky shot."

The boy turned and studied me with deep-set eyes. His eyebrows lifted. The beginnings of a grin turned up one corner of his mouth. He knows, I thought. I hadn't truly stumbled in that last second before launching the ball. I had realized, suddenly, that the ball was weighted, and I had shifted my shot accordingly. What the boy didn't know, and what brought my confidence roaring back, was that I had shot baskets under circumstances much worse— in the wind, the rain, and with every conceivable type of ball—apples, watermelons, balls of yarn, large stones. It was impossible to use Pete's ball every time I practiced. It would have been worn to its leather stitches.

We matched shots to five. The boy grunted and tossed the ball to me. "You lead, now," he said. I nodded and lined up a shot from the left corner. He matched my shots to ten. The crowd began to drift away. By fifteen the carnival worker cursed and stomped into his tent. At twenty-five, Ham was asleep, slumped against the legendary Cleopatra, a robed, heavily made-up middle-aged woman with a thick waist and dark hairs bristling from her chin. By thirty-five, it was just me, the carnival boy, and the ball. The song of night crickets played harmony to our thuds, grunts, and creaks.

The playing field was bathed in darkness. The lanterns had nearly all flickered out and the half-moon scuttled behind ragged clouds. The heat of the day had dissipated. I shivered in my shirtsleeves. Bennie had just wobbled in a matched shot of mine from way outside the original circle when something white and ghostly floated into the carnival grounds.

"Felix? Felix?" called a tremulous voice. "Where are you, Felix?"

Bennie tossed me the ball. I stood with it clutched to my chest, staring into the darkness. The hovering apparition moved toward us. Goosebumps tingled my arms. I held the ball closer and rubbed my right arm, trying to find some warmth.

"What's that?" I asked. My voice emerged in a whisper. I thought that perhaps the ghostly shape was one of the carnival freaks out for a late-night stroll.

"Felix? I can't see you. Are you there?" The specter moved closer. I suddenly realized the crickets had silenced.

"I don't know," Bennie replied. His voice was a whisper, too. He cleared his throat. "Your shot."

I dribbled the ball and tried to concentrate. I wanted to win so badly I could taste it.

I lined up to take my shot, a left-handed hook that I felt certain the right-handed Bennie would have trouble with. The white-cloaked figure moved closer.

"Felix? Oh, Felix." The tremulous voice was accompanied by a low huffing sound.

I paused and brought the ball back to my chest, trying to remember where I'd heard that sound before.

The figure continued to advance as if floating on air. "Felix?" Out of the gloom emerged the shape of a large, dark horse with a night-robed figure seated atop. But the recognition that one half of the ghostly figure was a horse didn't slow my beating heart. I noticed that Bennie stepped to the left as the horse moved closer. A pale white hand reached toward my face. I took an involuntary step back-ward.

The white figure slid from the horse and landed in front of me. I gasped.

"Oh! It's little Henry Soaring," the figure said. "Henry, have you seen my Felix?"

I froze. Henry was my father's name. "Noo," I said slowly. I wished someone would come to my rescue. Bennie or his father. Anyone. Then I took another look at the woman's face. "Mrs. Mortimer?" I asked incredulously. The woman was Abigail Mortimer, Ham's grandmother. At least, I thought it was. And the horse she held by a halter strap was Jalahar, AnnaLise's new colt. As if reading my mind, the colt snorted and shook his head. I held my breath and wondered how Mrs. Mortimer had managed to ride him. The colt was only half-broke.

"Yes, dear," she smiled, creasing deep wrinkles into her face. "Give your mother my regards, won't you, Henry? She certainly has her hands full keeping you out of trouble, doesn't she now? But I really must be going. If you see Felix, tell him to come home straightaway. I'm so very wor-ried about him." She lowered her voice. "He's been drink-ing again," she whispered. "The principal dismissed him from school, but he never came home."

I nodded, pretending to understand, and glanced ner-vously at the horse. He tossed his head. I could see the wild, rolling whites of his eyes and the mean flick of his ears. Mrs. Mortimer clung tenaciously to the halter, seemingly unaware of the horse's mad jerkings.

"Ham," I called over my shoulder to the sleeping figure, trying not to alarm the colt. "Ham! Wake up."

Bennie took my cue and nudged my best friend awake. The carnival worker peered out of his tent. "There is winner?"

"No, Papa," Bennie said. "Not yet."

"Bah!" the man said. He pulled his tent closed.

Mrs. Mortimer blinked at Bennie and the tents behind him, but the vacant smile stayed fixed to her face.

"Ham!" I called again. Then I grabbed Mrs. Mortimer by the hand and pulled her toward her grandson. The horse followed, stiff-legged. "Ham is here, Mrs. Mortimer. Can Ham help you?"

Ham looked around sleepily. "Is't time for the naked girl?" he mumbled as he staggered to his feet.

"Look, Ham. Look who's here," I said. "Your grand-mother. She's looking for Felix, only . . ." I bit my lower lip as I realized the Felix she was trying to find was still a boy.

Ham stared at his grandmother. "Granna? What are you doing here, Granna?" Ham turned to me, wild-eyed. "That's Jalahar," he said. "That horse is crazy."

As if to confirm, the horse started snorting and pawing the ground.

Mrs. Mortimer blinked at her grandson. "Have we met, dear?" she asked. "Are you one of Harry's little friends?"

I shivered. Somehow I knew that by Harry she must mean Harold—Harold Mortimer Senior, the Judge. No one else called Ham Harold except teachers.

"Granna! It's me, Ham. Your grandson. What are you doing at the carnival, Granna? It's the middle of the night."

Mrs. Mortimer looked around her, a puzzled look in

her eyes. "Where am I?" she whispered in a tiny voice. "Who are you?"

"Granna, I'm Ham, your grandson. It's me, Granna." Ham bit his bottom lip and then swiveled his head to stare wildly at me. "You gotta help me get her home. Sometimes, lately, she gets like this. You gotta help."

"I'm lost," said Mrs. Mortimer. Her voice sounded thin and reedy, like a child's. "I was picking blackberries on the hill and I got lost." Mrs. Mortimer began to wail. The sound shattered the night.

Jalahar whinnied and then reared. His hooves pierced the sky. Ham pushed his grandmother out of the way. "Grab the horse, Andy!" Ham yelled. Mrs. Mortimer continued to cry.

I stared at the flashing hooves and flying mane of the horse. The lead rope dangled from his halter. I gasped. If I didn't grab him just right, if I made a mistake . . . I took a step backward. The basketball stayed firmly tucked under my arm.

"Grab Jalahar!" Ham screamed again. Mrs. Mortimer's wails subsided to a low whimper.

It's AnnaLise's horse, I told myself firmly. Do it for AnnaLise. I tried to picture her smile of gratitude when I returned her horse, tried to imagine the light of thanks in her blue eyes, but I couldn't. All I could see were the horse's deadly hooves. I stayed frozen and trembling.

Jalahar thudded to the ground, planted his two front feet, and shook his head. I took another step backward, feeling like a coward, but too scared to do anything about it.

"Watch out," yelled a voice in my ear. "He's going to bolt!"

I cringed as the figure on my left launched itself toward the colt. Bennie grabbed the lead rope just as Jalahar reared. Bennie hung on grimly, bringing the horse back to earth. People began to emerge from the tents, surrounding the horse, crooning and whispering. Jalahar snorted, stamped, and finally settled.

"Who brings this horse in the night?" asked the carnival worker, who stood by Jalahar's head. His voice was low and soft, but there was no mistaking the underlying edge of accusation.

"It's . . . his," I said, pointing toward Ham, who was struggling to hold his grandmother steady.

The carnie glared at me and then looked at Bennie, who was still holding the horse's collar. "You win, no?" he asked his son.

Bennie shook his head. "It was a tie, Papa."

The man growled, causing Jalahar to flatten his ears. He patted the horse's neck and whispered something soothing. "Tie, bah," he said in the same low tones. "You play again."

I tried to swallow through the dry, gritty cotton of my mouth. "Er . . ." I began.

"We leave tomorrow, Papa," Bennie said. "Next town."

"You come back," Bennie's father said. "Stay with Teresa. Go to school."

"No!" Bennie said fiercely. Jalahar huffed. "No," he repeated softly.

Ham moved forward to take the rope from Bennie. I edged toward Mrs. Mortimer. She looked bewildered.

Bennie handed the rope to Ham. He looked at me, and then at the basketball. I tossed it to him.

"It was a tie," Bennie said. Then he turned and disappeared into one of the tents.

Ham led Jalahar forward. The horse followed with a dispirited flick of his tail. "Come on, Granna," Ham said. "Let's go home. Andy, help Granna."

I grabbed Mrs. Mortimer's frail, thin hand. She shuffled along next to me. "I was picking blackberries on the hill," she said. "You won't forget to get my blackberry bucket, will you?"

"Don't worry, Mrs. Mortimer. I'll get it," I said as we began the slow, strange walk through the darkened carnival toward town. I gave one last look at the peach basket. Twenty-five dollars, I thought wistfully. But in the morning the carnival would pack up and go. I felt a twinge of regret. I thought that if I'd been given the chance, I could have made friends with the carnival boy. I'd had more fun shooting baskets with him than with any of the other boys in town. But then I shrugged. I didn't guess I would ever see the boy or his basketball again.

Chapter Six

"Corn looks okay," Dad said as he sat down at the table. "Cold this morning, though."

I stared fuzzily at my breakfast and tried to stay awake.

"Do you think we'll get a freeze?" Mom's voice held a twinge of alarm that momentarily aroused my concentration. The threat of an early freeze cast fear into the heart of a farmer. We'd gotten an early freeze the year that Pete went off to war, I remembered. The corn had turned to mush in the fields. I'd always wondered if that freeze had something to do with Pete going away. My eyes drifted shut again as my parents' conversation floated around me.

"Andrew? Andrew!" I jolted awake to find my mother staring at me.

"Yes, ma'am?" I asked, trying desperately to recall what she had been talking about.

"I asked you if Ham had said anything."

My eyes widened. "Ham? I haven't seen Ham," I said quickly, ready to deny everything that had happened the night before. At my mother's puzzled expression, I asked, "Said anything about what?"

I could feel George looking at me. I tried to avoid his gaze. I had made it home with just enough time to grab my nightshirt from the chair, throw it into my dresser, and then sit on the edge of my bed, dressed and ready for chores. Except twice I had fallen asleep during milking, my head resting against the warm stomach of a cow. George had asked, more than once, why I was so tired.

"Said anything about his sister," Mother continued.

"AnnaLise? No. Why?" I asked, hoping that AnnaLise hadn't done anything to arouse my mother's displeasure. But AnnaLise couldn't do anything to make anyone mad. I imagined her long dark hair, her deep blue eyes, the dimple in her right cheek. I felt a silly grin start to spread across my face. Then I realized that both my parents were giving me funny looks. I shook my head and tried to clear it. I was having trouble following the conversation.

"About Claudia." Mother pursed her lips. "Has he said whether Claudia is coming home for the Centennial Picnic?"

"Oh." Claudia was Ham's oldest sister. Everybody had thought that she and Pete would get married. But after Pete died, Claudia moved to Chicago. She worked in one of the orphanages that Mother made blankets for. "No. He hasn't said anything," I replied.

The conversation drifted to other topics. My eyes began to close.

"Andrew, why don't you go to town with your father." She turned to my dad. "See if Mr. Malcolm will take the eggs in trade. I need a skein of wool and a five-pound bag of sugar."

"Hunh?" I snapped my head to attention. "What?"

"Andrew, are you feeling well?" Mother asked. She stared at me. "You look peaked, and you haven't eaten your porridge."

"He was up in the night," George tattled. I glared at him.

"I had to go to the privy," I said. "I'm fine."

Mother scrutinized my face. I opened my eyes wide and tried to look healthy. If I were declared sick, I'd be banished to my bed. I couldn't let that happen. I had things I needed to do. I had to practice my bank shot, and talk to Ham. We had to coordinate our stories, in case anyone saw us leading Mrs. Mortimer and Jalahar through town in the early hours of the morning. "I'm fine," I repeated.

"Then you won't mind taking some things to the Mortimers," Mother said firmly.

"Yes, ma'am." When Mother used that voice, I wasn't about to argue, even though I sometimes wondered why Mother never wanted to deliver her good works to the Mortimers herself.

After breakfast, I took off my overalls and changed into a clean pair of knickers and a shirt. They smelled like sunshine and Fels Naptha soap. I filled the washbowl with hot water from the stove, scrubbed my face, and slicked back my hair. Mother gave me a curious look as I washed up, but she didn't say anything. I didn't say anything, either.

I climbed into the front seat of the Model T and put the basket of blankets and Mother's eggs on the floorboard in front of me. Dad went around to the driver's side, reached over the wheel, and fiddled with the two rods that stuck out behind the steering wheel. Then he went to the front of the car, grabbed the choke wire with his left forefinger and the crank with his right hand. He pulled mightily.

The engine sputtered and died.

"You want me to mess with the rods while you pull the crank?" I asked.

"Don't touch them," Dad commanded.

Dad cranked again. The car sputtered and coughed, and then the motor caught. Dad jumped into the driver's seat, released the emergency brake, and shoved his foot against the low-speed pedal, and then we lurched out of the yard.

The trip to town was uneventful. The chugging of the motor and the bumping of the car over the gravel roads began to lull me to sleep. Vague images of basketballs and horses and naked ladies floated through my mind. I dreamed until the car stopped with a loud screech of brakes. We were at the town's only gasoline stand, parked next to the Red Crown gas tank. Ollie Hankerson looked up from under the hood of a four-cylinder Durant, waved a gray flannel rag, and strode toward us.

"Good day to fill 'er up," he said once he reached our car. Ollie always spoke with a lisp. He was missing his two front teeth. Mother said he lost them from chewing so much tobacco, but he told me he'd gotten them knocked out in a fight. He sometimes let me use his flat tire kit to patch and pump Pete's basketball. "Gas wars done reached Pierre. Price dropped to fifteen cents a gallon."

Dad furrowed his forehead. I could see him calculating how much a full tank would cost. Finally he nodded. "I need some oil, too." He turned to me. "Run along Andy, and don't forget the blankets. I'll take the eggs when I go to the grocer's."

I nodded, and climbed out of the car, but slowly. I liked to watch Ollie Hankerson pump the gas. He raised and lowered the long handle that was attached to the side of the red metal tank. The gasoline rose to the top of the clear glass container. Then he took the hose from the other side of the column and inserted it into the car. The liquid in the tank fell past the red marks that measured each gallon as it drained into our car.

I smelled the shimmering fumes of gasoline and thought about the day that I would own my own car. It wouldn't be an old Tin Lizzie, either. It would be something special because I was going to play basketball. I thought about the teams I had seen play in Bloomington: the Indianapolis Em-Roes and the Fort Wayne Caseys. Admission to the game cost a nickel, and the gym, which seated at least three thousand people, was always full. I wondered how many of those nickels the players got to keep. One day I'd find out.

I trudged down Holtsclaw Avenue, past the hardware store to the corner building that used to be a saloon but was now the Stone Mason Lodge. Mother had been glad when

Prohibition passed and all the saloons shut down. I guessed I was glad, too, because the Stone Masons nailed an iron basketball hoop to the side of their building. Sometimes I shot baskets there. I cut left through the lot that had parking for cars, now, along with the hitching posts for horses, and then ran across the street and toward the entrance to Sanders Stone Mill. The doors to the building were wide open, so I walked in, my ears immediately assaulted by the rasp of metal grinding against stone. I took a deep breath. The mill smelled like nothing else I knew, pungent and damp. It made me think of a picture I'd seen once of the ocean pounding against a rocky beach. I thought the ocean must smell a lot like a limestone mill.

"Hey, Andy, whadd'ya bring me?" Teddy Turpin, the planerman, ground his huge cutting tool to a stop against the stanchion. He pointed toward the basket.

"They're blankets. For the Mortimers," I said with a shrug.

Gene Swango let loose a loud wolf whistle. He looped a woven belt around a large, polished block so the traveling crane could lift it across the mill. He paused and leaned against the stone. "Them Mortimers got a lot of pretty little girls. You gone and got yourself a girlfriend?"

Frank Koblin, the crane man, groaned. "Naw, Andy, say it ain't so. Them dames is nothing but trouble."

I made a face to hide my embarrassment. I wished I'd hidden the basket outside. "It's from my mom," I said by way of explanation. "Hey, Cal, where's that one going?" I pointed to the rock that Gene was hooking to the crane.

Cal, the car blocker, laughed at my question, but he walked over and checked a mark on the side of the stone. "Washington, D.C.," he said. "They're building a church or some such out that'a'way."

I nodded. I liked to imagine what happened to the stone once it left the quarry or the mill. Cal said Indiana limestone practically built the city of Indianapolis, and that they sent stones as far away as Chicago and New York City.

A tiny, wizened man wearing a fedora and a bow tie beckoned me toward the corner where he sat. "You been carving?" he asked in a voice barely loud enough to hear.

I took a nervous breath, but pulled a small lump of stone from my pocket and handed it to him. He pursed his lips as one finger traced the lines etched into the stone. It had taken me a dozen stones and a lot of weeks of pounding and chiseling, but I finally had something I wasn't reluctant to show him. It was a basketball swishing through a hoop. The crisscross lines of the net were the toughest to get just right.

He handed the stone back to me. "Not bad," he said. "Want to start a new one?"

I nodded. I had hoped he would ask.

He reached behind him, toward a stack of limestone blocks about the size of my fist. He fiddled and sorted for a moment, and then finally pulled one toward him. "This one," he said, after studying it for a moment. He handed it to me.

I felt the smooth, satisfying weight of the stone. "Thank you, sir," I said.

He stared at me. "You aim to be a carver when you grow up?"

I grinned at the compliment, but I knew he was joshing me. The carvers were the most respected men in town and this man, Jeremiah Donegol, was the best.

"Heck, how 'bout now?" Gene asked. "We got more work than we got men. You want a job, you tell that foreman I gave you the okay."

I knew there were kids who left school after the eighth grade to work in the quarries, but I shook my head. "I aim to play basketball," I said. "Take Pierre High School to the state finals. When I grow up, maybe I'll go to Indianapolis and play for the Em-Roes."

The stone men erupted into laughter. Gene Swango marched over and slapped me on the back. "You do that, Andy, my boy. You do that. And when they decide to build a massive gymnasium for you to play in, we'll cut the stone for ya'."

The men chuckled. I laughed along with them, but I wasn't joking.

"All right, boys, enough loafing," the foreman hollered. "This stone ain't going to cut itself. Get back to work!"

The cacophony of saws and hammers resumed. I skipped out, shaking the limestone dust from my hair and blowing it off my carving. If something awful happened that made it so I couldn't play basketball, maybe I would be a carver.

But there wasn't any reason to think about working at the mill, I told myself as I walked toward the Mortimers' house on the hill. I'd never stop playing basketball. I gave a little whoop and jumped into the air.

Chapter Seven

Ham was still in bed when I knocked on his door at eleven o'clock that morning. "Poor boy, I think he might have a touch of cold," Mrs. Mortimer said as she opened the door to her Georgian mansion. "You are welcome to go up, just don't get too close, Andrew, darling. I wouldn't want you to take sick on our account."

"Thank you, ma'am," I said as I slid past her. "But I don't reckon I'll catch anything."

"No, you're right. Not a strong, healthy boy like you." She smiled at me in that vacant, somewhere-else way she had. She reminded me of a butterfly. She flitted here and there, not really accomplishing much of anything, but it didn't seem to matter. Everyone still smiled when they saw her.

I handed her the basket. "These are from Mother," I said. "For Claudia's orphanage."

"Oh, thank you!" Mrs. Mortimer beamed. "Claudia will be pleased. Your mother really is a saint, Andrew. I don't know how she does it all. Send her my regards, won't you?"

"Yes, ma'am."

Mrs. Mortimer fluttered off. I watched her for a moment. The Mortimers and my family had been friends since my dad and the Judge were little boys. But when Pete went off to war, the two families stopped visiting. Everyone except Ham and me.

I took my time walking up the wide, oak stairway. I wondered if AnnaLise was home. I wondered if maybe *she* was still in bed. My stomach gave a funny little flip. I bolted up the last three steps and ran down the hallway to Ham's room.

Ham was sitting on the floor next to his bed. He was wearing a pair of headphones and was fiddling with wires wrapped around two boxes of Quaker Oats.

"Ham," I called. "Ham!"

Ham glanced up and smiled. "I got it working," he said loudly. "Isn't it keen?"

I nodded. Ham had been working on this crystal radio set since the newspaper printed an article about how to build one. "Can you hear anything?" I asked.

He shrugged. "I'm getting a station out of Chicago," he said. "But all they're playing is opera." He wrinkled his nose and removed the headphones. He walked to his bed and flopped down on it.

"I'm exhausted," he said. "Mom thinks I'm sick, but

really, I just couldn't get out of bed. What a night we had, hunh?"

I raised my eyebrows and folded my arms across my chest. "We had? What a night *we* had?"

Ham shrugged. "How was I to know you were going to get into an all-night shoot-out with that carnival kid? All I wanted to do was see a naked lady and then go home." He snapped his fingers. "But you had to go and prove yourself—"

"Oh, be quiet, Ham." I sank down onto his bed. I desperately longed to lay my head on one of those fluffy pillows and fade into sleep.

Ham yawned. He sipped orange juice from a glass on his nightstand. "Wasn't last night swell?" he asked. "The way you nearly won all that money just from shooting baskets?"

I tried not to think about the money. With twenty-five dollars I could have bought a crystal radio for myself. The year before, a radio station had broadcast a basketball game. I wished I could have heard it. Still, I'd almost won. The memory made me smile. "Yeah, swell," I said. "How's your grandmother?"

Ham's face went blank. "Fine," he said. He picked up a comic and started leafing through it.

"But is she—"

"She's fine!" Ham repeated. "She's resting."

I glanced uneasily around the room while Ham flipped rapidly through his comic. "She called me Henry."

"So? What of it?"

I shrugged. "Well . . ." I lowered my voice. "That's my father's name. She thought *I* was my father. When he was a boy. It was kind of . . . screwy."

"Just shut up about it!" Ham hollered. "Who cares what she called you? Maybe she should have called you a chicken-face."

I watched as Ham blinked his eyes rapidly. Then I turned away and pretended to study a crack on the wall. Ham loved his granna. He used to say that she was the only person in his entire family who really loved him. She was the only person who understood when he did something stupid, the only person he could talk to about it. But I suddenly realized that he hadn't talked about his granna in a long time.

"Well . . ." I cleared my throat. "I guess it was a good thing we went to the carnival. Because we found her." I paused. "And if anyone saw us out last night, we could just say that we were looking for her."

"Yeah . . ." Ham said quietly. "We could say that."

I was working up my courage to ask Ham if AnnaLise was home when the door to his room burst open.

"Harold Andrew!" AnnaLise barged in. "You are the laziest, no good—"

"Good morning to you, too," Ham said.

"Hi, AnnaLise," I said. My voice squeaked.

AnnaLise looked at me and smiled, flashing her dimple. "Hi, Andy. I didn't know you were here."

I nodded, feeling dumb. I sidled close to the wall and tried to wipe away the moisture that had suddenly appeared on my palms. I had never given AnnaLise a second thought before this summer. She had always been Ham's pesky little sister. But all of a sudden she was different, somehow.

AnnaLise directed her attention back to her brother. "I understand that you're sick."

Ham coughed into his hand. Then he shook his head weakly. "Feel so bad—"

"Why you, you. . . !" AnnaLise clenched her fists by her sides and stomped her foot.

"What's wrong?" I asked, finally finding my voice. "What did he do?"

"The Judge arranged for him to help Mrs. Pickens sort through the newspaper archives today," AnnaLise said. "It's his restitution."

I glanced at Ham. His face was blank. I looked back at AnnaLise. She glowered. "Remember?" she asked. "Remember how you snuck into the printing press and changed the newspaper masthead from *Pierre Journal* to *Privy Journey?*"

Ham's mouth twitched. I tried to hide my grin. I remembered him telling me about that. Ten papers had been printed with the new masthead before the newspaper editor caught the change. Ham had tried to keep one, but Mrs. Pickens had them all burned.

Ham bowed his head. "I am so sorry about that," he said. I could hear the laughter in his voice. "I promised that I'd make it up to her."

"But now that you're *sick,* Mother said that I have to go in your place!" AnnaLise looked close to tears. "I'll miss my training session with Jalahar."

"How is Jalahar this morning?" Ham asked. I whipped around to stare at him, but his face was void of expression.

"He's fine," AnnaLise said. She paused for a moment. "In fact, he's almost calm. His training must be working." Her voice began to rise again. "But that's why I have to work with him! I don't have time to spend all day at the newspaper office." Her voice sounded desperate. Her blue eyes were moist, and twin spots of color had appeared on her cheeks.

"I'll go," I blurted. AnnaLise and Ham both turned and stared at me.

"You'll go where?" they asked in unison.

"I'll . . ." I cleared my throat. "I'll go to the newspaper office for you."

Ham raised his eyebrows. "You will?" He nodded. "See, AnnaLise? Andy's going to help. He understands about a person being sick."

If AnnaLise hadn't been there I would have punched him. But that was the problem. AnnaLise and her dimple were making me do things I would otherwise have never done in a thousand years.

AnnaLise turned to me and smiled. "You're really sweet, Andy. Come on, I'll walk with you."

I forgot about the carnival, I forgot about Ham's grand-mother, and I forgot about my plans to shoot baskets that afternoon. I blissfully let AnnaLise lead me down the stairs and out the door toward the domain of Mabel Pickens, newspaper editor and self-proclaimed town historian.

Chapter Eight

I walked reluctantly into the newspaper office, with Anna-Lise by my side. Mrs. Pickens ran the town newspaper, the town library, and the town historical society. If there was something to know about Pierre, Indiana, she knew it. There were rumors that she was half crazy.

The front room of the newspaper office was tiny. Floor-to-ceiling bookcases lined the walls. Boxes were piled knee-high and newsprint covered a long table at the end of the room. Another table and a couple of chairs stood in the middle of the room. I took a deep breath and inhaled the pungent smell of ink and the woodsy smell of paper. We had only been there a moment when Mabel Pickens bustled through the side door. As she entered I heard the roar of the printing press churning out Saturday's copies of the *Pierre Journal.* Mabel Pickens slammed the door behind her and looked us over. She was tiny and chipper like a mischievous elf. I tried not to stare. She was dressed in the most peculiar outfit I had ever seen. Her blouse was blue and crinkly, with a high lace collar and puffy sleeves, like something out of a history book. But on the bottom she wore knickers. I blinked. Not bloomers, which she had been known to wear out in public, but knickers. Boys' knickers. And over everything she wore a big canvas apron covered with inkblots.

"Neither of you are Harold Mortimer Junior," she stated.

"No, ma'am," AnnaLise and I answered. I risked a glance at AnnaLise out of the corner of my eye. She had her eyes firmly fixed on the floor.

"And where is Ham, since you are not he?" she asked.

"He's . . ." I began.

"Sick . . ." AnnaLise muttered.

"Hmmph." Mrs. Pickens stared at me over the tops of her spectacles. "Meaning physically ill. Derived from the Old English."

"Yes, ma'am," I said, even though I had no idea what she was talking about.

We waited for a moment. AnnaLise started to fidget. "Well, thanks, Andy. Good-bye!" AnnaLise turned and flew out the door. Mrs. Pickens and I watched her go in silence.

Once she had gone, Mrs. Pickens clapped her hands together and steered me toward the first stack of boxes. "Let's get moving, then, young man." She reminded me of the Wiltshires' border collie. He'd herd sheep, ducks, geese, cows, the Wiltshire children, anything. One Sunday he got into the church and herded the grammar school choir from the rehearsal room to the sanctuary and back again.

"Isn't this exciting? Pierre, Indiana, will soon be celebrating its centennial. One hundredth anniversary. From the Latin *centum.*"

"Yes, ma'am." Mrs. Pickens was the only one in town who pronounced the name of our town *Pee-air,* as if she were speaking French. Everybody else said *Perry.* She was also the only person I knew who talked like Noah Webster's dictionary.

"Start with this box. Sort through the clippings, classify them according to date, event, and person and stack them in proper order," she said.

A border collie in knickers.

I shifted the contents of the box onto the table and stared in dismay at the heaps of dusty, yellowing newspaper clippings. I sighed. Ham was home reading comics. *Privy Journey* indeed. It was his fault I was here. His and AnnaLise's. Frank Koblin from the mill was right. Girls were nothing but trouble.

I began the tedious process of scanning, sorting, reading, and writing. This would take all afternoon. Mrs. Pickens scurried back and forth between the bookshelves, the table, and the printing press. Every time she opened the door the noise from the press rattled the shelves. "Nearly finished with tomorrow's edition," she yelled as she closed the door behind her.

I nodded. "Yes'm."

Mrs. Pickens pulled another box toward me without

breaking stride. "Here we go then," she said in her rapid-fire voice. "Let's not dawdle."

Verb, I thought. To waste time.

"Hey, look at this," I exclaimed, holding up an article. "This is a story about that basketball game between the Caseys and the Celtics." I scanned the story about the game that had taken place in Fort Wayne last March. I thought the story was dry as sawdust. It didn't even mention how monumental it was that the Caseys beat the legendary Celtics.

"Did you know that it cost a dollar fifty to get into the game? And it was sold out! The Caseys were unstoppable. Stonebraker was hitting shots from fifty feet out. The Celtics didn't even guard him because they didn't think anybody could hit from out there. And the Caseys' defense shut down the Celtics' center, Dutch Dehnert. Dutch didn't score a single point!"

"Did you attend the game?" Mrs. Pickens asked, looking at me over her spectacles.

"No, ma'am. I read about it, though."

"I see," Mrs. Pickens said. "Continue, please."

I wasn't ready to admit that this was interesting, but as I sorted, I looked for more articles about basketball. I came across an article about the engagement of Claudette Snodgrass—I chuckled over her last name—to Harold Mortimer. "Hey, I never knew Mrs. Mortimer was from Hog's Hollow," I exclaimed as I read. "That's where my mother was born." I clamped my mouth shut as soon as I heard the words leave my lips. Mother hated Hog's Hollow. She would never admit, not to anyone, where she had grown up.

It wasn't even a town, really, just an old quarry camp somewhere between Oolitic and Needmore.

Mrs. Pickens didn't change expression. She probably already knew my mother was from Hog's Hollow. Since she was the newspaper editor, I guessed Mrs. Pickens knew most everything.

The next several boxes were filled with announcements—weddings, deaths, and births. I sorted and filed and started to feel like I was snooping into other people's business. I guessed the announcement about Pete's death was in one of those boxes. I hoped I wouldn't find it.

On one of the clippings, my father's name caught my eye. I scanned it quickly. It was the announcement of my parents' wedding—the betrothal of Henry Soaring and Beatrice Hite. There was no mention of Hog's Hollow. But, "this can't be right," I mumbled. "This says they were married on February 14, 1900."

Mrs. Pickens hurried toward me and peered over my shoulder. "Of course it's right," she said quickly. "My facts are always correct."

"But they were married in December," I said. "Before the turn of the century." I frowned. December was the month written in the family Bible.

The rattle from next door came to a stop. The sudden silence was deafening. I looked up from the wedding announcement. "I'd better go check on the paper," Mrs. Pickens said. "Either the print run is finished or Father has broken the press. Why don't you run along now, Andrew. Thank you for your help."

I sighed with relief and raced to the door, but not

before noticing that Mrs. Pickens had taken the wedding announcement from the pile and tucked it into a pocket on her apron. I shook my head. There were a lot of things that I still didn't understand about grown-ups.

I knew Dad hadn't waited for me, so I walked home slowly, my feet automatically taking me through the cemetery. I skirted headstones both plain and elaborately carved, instinctively reciting the names of those on the stones. A rasping noise in that normally silent place caught me off guard, and I stopped in the shade of an ancient oak.

A figure stood in front of Pete's grave, hammering and grinding the headstone. I waited and watched from the shadows. It was Dad. Over the last five years he had chipped into the bulky stone so that now it resembled an eagle, wings stretched as if ready to take flight. Dad was carving the last details with an old-fashioned chisel. I stared in silence. Dad never talked about Pete, but he sure spent a lot of time working on that headstone. Only after Dad had packed up his tools and driven away in the clanking Model T did I move from my spot. I walked to the headstone and ran my fingers over its intricate surface. I had wondered, when Pete's headstone was first laid, why the limestone block was so big and the print at the bottom so little. Now it made sense. The lettering read:

PETER ELIJAH SOARING
August 14, 1900–November 11, 1918
A Son of God's Mercy
Soaring on Wings of Eagles

I traced the dates with my forefinger. Pete had just turned seventeen when he left for the war. Three years older than I was now. It wasn't right. He'd been too young. He'd had to lie to get into the army.

"You shouldn't have left!" I yelled at the statue. I stared at the headstone for a moment. "You shouldn't have died!"

I turned away and started the two-mile journey back to the farm. As I walked, I dribbled an imaginary basketball and wondered if I'd ever be able to take his place.

Chapter Nine

I spent the next two weeks working in the fields. I slogged through the long, hot days, trying not to think about Pete or basketball or AnnaLise. But the more I tried not to think, the more I thought. I had checked the family Bible, and the date of Mother and Dad's wedding was just the same as I'd thought—December 14, 1899. Mrs. Pickens had been wrong after all. "Gee up, Jemmy! Get on, Jo-Jo!" I flicked the reins over the backs of the horses, but they just twitched their ears and plodded forward.

Some of the old-time farmers talked about their draft horses like they were children, but I thought that horses, all horses, were smelly, stupid, and mean-tempered. Dad had fixed the tractor, but he said it was only for big jobs. He told me to use Jemmy and Jo-Jo to pull the cultivator.

Dust and gnats rose into the air as I passed, covering me with a fine layer of grime. I hawed the horses and felt them move forward in their traces. Sweat beaded on my forehead and ran in itchy rivulets down my back.

"Move, you dumb animals!" I called. I looked at the sun in the sky, guessing it to be midafternoon. Monday was Labor Day, which meant the Pierre Centennial Picnic with its annual free-throw contest. This year I wanted to win, which was why my basketball was lashed on top of Jemmy and Jo-Jo's harness.

I groaned as I turned Jemmy and Jo-Jo. I was working in the westernmost field, which bordered the edge of our property. Ahead in the distance I could see the old, rusted derrick that still stood sentry over the old Vigo Quarry. I knew that being a quarrier wasn't any easier than being a farmer. Pulling stones from the ground was just as tough as growing corn in it, but I sometimes wondered what it would be like if we were a stone family again. Everyone in town bragged that the country was on a building spree, and limestone was running at full capacity. Prices were rising. Not like corn, which we couldn't seem to give away. I'd heard Dad worry aloud whether the corn would even pay for itself this year, much less the mortgage.

But the land Granddad bought didn't have limestone, I reminded myself as I turned the horses away from the site of the derrick and toward the last edge of the field. That was the trouble. Granddaddy had invested everything we had in buying the land and clearing it. He had even put in a railroad spur. But the promised limestone wasn't there.

I stopped at the edge of the field and inhaled the sweet fragrance of sun-baked dirt and fresh corn. Jo-Jo whickered and Jemmy pawed the ground. I untied my basketball, unbuckled their traces, and heaved off the yoke. I tied long reins to a sapling, and then slapped Jemmy on the rump. The horses meandered into the clover alongside the trees and began to graze. I cut through a field of scrubby wood toward an old shack that hunched the edge of our property. It was a quarryier's shack. The land it was on stuck like a finger from our property into Vigo land, where the Italian stonecutters lived. Daddy didn't farm that finger of land, and I don't think anybody knew this shack was even here. I had turned it into my hideout. Several years ago I had nailed an iron hoop ten feet up on the side of the weathered wall. I took another glance at the sun. Plenty of time before I had to get the horses to the barn and myself to the supper table.

I paced the distance to the free-throw spot and drew a line in the dirt with my shoe. I held the basketball in front of me, eyed the basket, bent my knees, and launched it. The ball sailed through the hoop without a rattle. I rebounded the ball, returned to the line, and shot again.

Ten in a row. I grinned. The two weeks without practice hadn't hurt as much as I'd feared. Fifteen. A loud pop just as I aimed number sixteen caused me to lose my concentration. The ball bounced off the edge of the hoop and ricocheted into the woods.

I retrieved the ball and searched for the cause of the sound. There was a low rumble of an automobile and a thick plume of dust on the dirt road that led to the Vigo Quarry. I walked back to the shack with my ball under my arm and watched. Who was coming to the quarry? Everybody knew it was too dangerous to swim in, and the limestone had tapped out several years before.

The car didn't stop at the quarry. It kept on, bumping over a rutted dirt road toward the shack. I ducked behind the building, but not before glancing toward the horses. They were too far away, I decided, to take notice of the automobile.

A sleek, silver Packard stopped in front of the shack. The car doors opened and two men emerged. My eyes widened in surprise. It was Sheriff Mortimer and Dad. I started to call out, but something about the look on Dad's face made me stop.

Felix Mortimer was dressed all in black—black over-coat, black trilby, even black-rimmed goggles. He removed the goggles, wiped his face with a handkerchief, and then slowly removed the overcoat and placed it on the driver's seat. Underneath the coat he wore a black suit with his silver star pinned to it.

Dad looked like he always looked—worn bib overalls, worn work shirt, worn set to his massive shoulders.

They walked toward the shack. I moved to the side of the building, where a large knothole in one of the boards let me see what was going on inside.

"How's the corn crop look this year?" I heard the sheriff ask as they opened the door. It creaked but opened wide enough to let them walk inside.

The shack was bare except for a few stacks of wooden boxes. There was enough light from the doorway and the cracks in the ceiling that I could see Dad and Sheriff Mortimer through my knothole.

"It'll be fine, if the weather holds until harvest," Dad said.

"What's the bushel price?" the sheriff asked.

I heard Dad make a strange sort of noise in the back of his throat. "Don't worry, Felix. You'll get your money."

"I hear some folks are using corn to ferment their own cash crop," the sheriff said. "To supplement their income, so to speak." His voice had a strange sound to it.

"I'm not the one brewing the moonshine!" Dad replied. "I don't know where those drunks at the jail are getting their alcohol, but it's not from me."

"Oh, no, of course it's not you. I wasn't even suggesting." The sheriff walked around the shack. I pulled away from the knothole when he passed. "I think I've got a good idea of who's abiding by the law of Prohibition and who isn't. It's those Italians that take some watching. I'm surprised you let them live as close as they do."

"Fine people. Some of the best stonecutters in the country," Dad mumbled.

"Catholics," Felix replied.

"Did you bring me all the way out here to talk about my neighbors' religion?" Dad asked. "Because I got a lot of work to do to get the harvest in."

"No, no." Felix held up his hands. His tiepin, an oddly-shaped cross of silver, flashed in the sun that streamed in from the cracks in the wall. "Sorry, just making conversation. The reason I brought you out here is because I have a business proposition. I'd like to buy this bit of land from you."

I wished I could see Dad's face, to see if he looked as shocked as I felt. Sheriff Mortimer wasn't a farmer. What did he want with our land? With my hideout?

"Just a couple of acres, five at the most. From here, um, north to the Possum River . . ."

"West to Possum River," Dad said. I grinned, thinking about Ham's lack of directional sense. It must run in the family. "But I don't own that land. This quarter-acre strip is all I own for about two hundred yards. Where Splashing Creek splits with Possum River starts the edge of my seventy-five acres. And I can't sell that acreage. I'm farming every spare bit of land I can."

"Oh." Felix rubbed his chin. "But not this?" He spun around in a slow circle.

"Too narrow. Too rocky," Dad said.

"But who owns that land?" Felix asked, waving vaguely in the direction of the river.

"Bert and Judson Crowley, I reckon," Dad said. "Most of the land to the west of Vigo belongs to the Crowleys." Dad paused. "You don't aim to start farming, do you?"

"Farming?" Felix looked puzzled. "Oh! Oh, no. I just wanted a getaway. You know, a place to do a little hunting, a little fishing."

Dad shrugged, and once again I wished I could see his face through my peephole. "I'll have to think it over," he said. "This land has always been in the family. I'd sure consider it, though, if I could lower some of that mortgage. In fact I'd be grateful. Otherwise I'll have to sell the tractor. But if you want to buy any more than this little strip, you have to talk to Bert and Judson."

Felix nodded, but he looked distracted, like he was already thinking of something else. "Bert might want to sell some of the land," Felix said. "Since Judson's moving to Indianapolis."

I sat back in surprise. Coach Crowley? Moving?

"To Indianapolis?" Dad asked. "Judson?"

"He was offered a job coaching basketball at one of the Indianapolis high schools. They're going to pay him well, I heard. And you know he's never liked farming," Felix said.

A job in Indianapolis? But who would coach the Pierre Carvers? Who would take us to the state championship?

I eased myself away from the shack and raced through the woods without waiting for Sheriff Mortimer and my father to finish their conversation. I sprinted to the field where George was detasseling corn.

"Coach Crowley—moving to Indianapolis!" I gasped as soon as I was within shouting distance.

George turned to me. "What?" he asked irritably. "Where are Jemmy and Jo-Jo? You'd better be done with the cultivating because I'm not doing it for you. I don't know how you weaseled out of the detasseling, but—"

"Blast!" I muttered. I had forgotten about the horses. But this was more important. "Coach Crowley! He took a job in Indianapolis!" I repeated. I stood in front of my brother and tried to catch my breath. "I heard it just now."

"Oh, just stop it, Andy." George glared at me as if this was another of my pranks, but I nodded furiously.

"It's true. I heard Sheriff Mortimer tell Dad!" I didn't know how many times I'd have to say it before I finally convinced him.

"Indianapolis?" George still sounded disbelieving. "Why would he do a thing like that? It's my senior year!"

"Another school offered him more money."

George looked as upset as I had ever seen him. He had every right to be, I thought. Coach Crowley operated on the seniority mentality. Those who put in their time and followed his rules through the four years of high school earned a right to play, regardless of their skill level. I guessed George was worried that a new coach might do things differently. But the idea of a new coach didn't thrill me, either. At least I knew what to expect from Coach Crowley.

"Come on, let's go get washed up for supper," George said.

"I gotta get the horses."

"The horses? You mean you haven't put them up already? Where were you, when you heard Sheriff Mortimer tell Dad about Coach?" George demanded. "Were you eavesdropping?"

George said the word *eavesdropping* like the Anti-Saloon League might have said *drinking*. I rolled my eyes. "Come on. They're not far." My mind raced with questions. "I wonder who will coach us? When does the school board meet again? Do you think they have someone picked out already?"

We put the horses away and hurried to the house for supper. I knew, and George knew, too, that supper was the best time to get Dad talking about what the sheriff had said. We couldn't come right out and ask him about Coach Crowley because he'd know I'd been listening. I was pretty sure Dad and Sheriff Mortimer hadn't intended for anyone to be skulking around that old shack. But George and I could at least try to steer the conversation in the direction of Coach Crowley. It was absolutely crucial that we find out what was going on. The entire basketball season was at stake, along with everything I'd been hoping for.

Chapter Ten

"School'll be starting soon," George said as soon as Dad finished with the prayer. "In two weeks." George looked at me with raised eyebrows. I guessed I could have thought of a better way to get the conversation steered toward basketball, but I nodded and got ready to play along.

Dad grunted as he fiddled with placing his napkin on his lap. Mother always made us mess with linens at suppertime. She wanted us to learn etiquette. "We need to load the rest of the hay into the barn," he said dourly. "We'll have to harvest the corn early if the temperature keeps dropping."

"Will we get an early freeze?" Mother asked. She placed a bowl of green beans on the table, and then sat down.

"The corn will be fine," I said quickly. "We'll be done with the hay and the vegetables by the time school starts. Then it'll be basketball season." I looked at George. He didn't smile.

"What did Walter say at the grain mill?" Mother asked. Walter Tuglin was considered the local expert on all things corn.

"Thinks we should be in good shape if we get the corn shucked by the first of October," Dad said. He scooped a pile of beans into his mouth. I waited anxiously while he chewed. "But the way the prices keep dropping, doesn't see as it does us much good. Haven't been this low since before the war."

"Will we keep it all for the animals, then?" Mother asked. She cut a tiny piece of pork chop and chewed on it daintily.

George made a choking sound. I hunted for something to say to change the subject. My parents could talk about corn and the weather all night.

"I thought I saw Sheriff Mortimer's Packard when I was working in the western field," I said quickly. George stared at me and raised his hands out to his sides.

Mother frowned. "What was he doing out there?"

"Just passing through," Dad said. "Keeping an eye on things." He scooped a forkful of mashed potatoes and shoved them into his mouth. George groaned.

"Are you ill?" Mother asked him. George shook his head.

"George and I were talking about school before," I said, trying to get the conversation moving in the right direction. "We were thinking that Coach Crowley was probably going to get after us with calisthenics, and such. He sure is a stickler about calisthenics, Coach Crowley is."

George sighed and sat back in his chair. We both stared

at Dad. He didn't respond. He seemed to be figuring something in his head.

"Don't you think so, Dad?" George prompted.

"What's that?" Dad asked absentmindedly.

"That Coach Crowley is a stickler about calisthenics! Don't you think he'll get us in good shape before the basketball season starts?"

"I suppose." Dad said. He ate another forkful of mashed potatoes. George and I stared at one another.

You are a liar, George mouthed. I shook my head rapidly. I knew what I'd heard.

We ate in silence for a moment. "Sure am looking forward to basketball," I said.

"I've been meaning to talk to you about the western corner of our property, Beatrice—"

"Yep, basketball will be great!" I yelled. I lifted myself up in my seat. "So great!"

Mother and Dad both turned and stared at me in astonishment. Mother set her mouth in a tight line. "Guess I'm pretty excited," I said, this time more softly. I settled back into my chair. "Sorry for interrupting."

"Don't get too excited, Andy," George said. "Coach Crowley doesn't play freshmen."

"I heard today that Coach Crowley is moving to Indianapolis," Dad said. He turned his attention away from me and back to his plate.

"Moving to Indianapolis?" I asked.

"But he can't move," George said. "Who'll coach the basketball team?"

"The school board will find a replacement," Dad said. "I expect we'll be hearing about it in the *Pierre Journal*. Basketball's too important to this town to be without a coach for long. I imagine they already have someone in mind."

"But who?" I asked. "Who are they going to get?"

Dad shrugged. "I'm sure they'll find somebody. Now, finish up your dinner. Cows need to be bedded down and the hogs fed."

We ate quietly for a few minutes, and then mother asked, "Henry, what were you saying about the land?"

I gulped my food and raced for the door. "I'll slop the hogs," I yelled. On my way to the pigsty I scooped my basketball under my arm. If we were getting a new coach, I needed to practice even more.

Chapter Eleven

On Monday morning I woke early. After milking the cows and gathering eggs I filled the washbowl and scrubbed my face and arms with soap. I splashed them clean and peered at my face in the cracked mirror. Dad's new Gillette Safety Razor was on the shelf, next to his shaving lather. I rubbed my chin, contemplating.

"What are you doing?" George asked as he walked past the washstand.

"Nothing!" I quickly dried my face, and then went to our room to dress. I put on my second-best corduroy knickers with a starched white shirt, suspenders, and a bow tie. I gave my basketball a lucky pat, put some marbles in my pocket, and adjusted my cap.

As soon as we were ready, Dad drove us into town. We joined some other cars on the road along with a couple of horses and buggies. The horses pulled to the side as we passed. A banner was strung across Main Street that announced "One Hundred Years in Pierre—1823–1923." When we drove under the banner, everyone began honking their horns, waving, and hollering. Even Mother had a smile on her face.

I helped Mother deliver her pies, and then I found Ham. He was playing marbles with a couple of other boys from town.

I knelt down and began to play.

"Betcha a nickel I can knock out your blue glassie," Ham said as he took aim.

I didn't have time to tell him I hadn't had so much as a penny. He flicked his marble. It rolled across the dirt, but stopped short of my glassie.

"Awww." A couple of the boys laughed, but Ham grinned, stood, and pulled a coin out of his pocket. He flipped it to me. I stared at it for a minute. "You giving this to me?" I asked.

"You won it, didn't you?"

I looked at the nickel, shrugged, and then pocketed it.

"Come on," Ham said. "Let's go look at the cars."

Some of the men had brought their cars, polished and shined to a mirror finish, and parked them on the lawn of the First United Methodist Church. There were half a dozen Model T's, a brand-new Hudson, two Cadillacs, Sheriff Mortimer's Packard, and a Marmon Model 34 Speedster.

"I'd like one of those," Ham said. "Boy, they're fast."

We walked toward the new fire truck and ogled it for a minute. It was big, gasoline powered, and painted a shiny red. A large bell hung on the top. Mr. Bickner clanged the bell, and waved. When he wasn't being a firefighter, Mr. Bickner worked for the railroad, loading limestone and corn into boxcars and shipping it across the United States. I waved back.

"Hey, look it." Ham pointed. "There's my mom and my sisters." Ham laughed.

I turned quickly. "AnnaLise?" I asked.

"Yeah. Mom made them make box lunches for the raffle, even AnnaLise." He shook his head. "I pity the poor fool that buys *her* lunch."

I stared across the park to the table where the women were setting up for the box lunch raffle. My heart started pounding. I reached into my pockets, pulled out the contents, and studied it—twelve marbles, a ripped movie stub, a chew of gum, and the nickel I'd won from Ham. I bit my lower lip.

"You want to go look the lunches over?" I asked. "See what looks good?"

Ham frowned and shook his head. "Uh-uhn."

"Aren't you gonna buy a lunch?" I asked, shoving everything back in my pocket.

Ham shook his head. "Not from some girl, anyway. Mom packed enough in her box for me and the Judge. Why? Are you gonna buy one?"

I shrugged. "I dunno. Maybe." I took a deep breath and imagined eating lunch with AnnaLise. "Depends how hungry I am, I guess." I stuck my hand in my pockets and began to whistle. "Hey," I asked. "You want to play some more marbles? I'll bet you your nickel that I can knock out your Donneck on my first try."

Ham grinned and punched me in the shoulder. "That's the spirit. Who cares about a bunch of girls and their lunches, anyway?"

We played marbles for two hours, except for the twenty minutes we stopped to watch the parade. Some of the other boys joined in. By lunchtime I had lost five glassies and an agate, but I had won four pennies, two quarters, and a buffalo nickel. I was starving.

I scanned the table, trying to guess which box belonged to AnnaLise. I certainly couldn't ask Ham. He'd think I'd gone plumb crazy. Maybe I had, I thought, as I studied each box for a clue. There were a lot to choose from.

"Hi, Andy." My stomach flipped at the sound of Anna-Lise's voice behind me. "What are you doing?"

I shoved my hands in my pockets and tried to look nonchalant. "Oh, nothing," I said. I turned around to smile at her.

I blinked in disbelief. AnnaLise was standing there, but she wasn't alone. Next to her stood the kid from the carnival.

"Hey," we both exclaimed at the same time.

"Do you two know each other?" AnnaLise asked.

"No!" I said quickly. I stared at him, trying to figure out what he was doing there. The carnival had left town weeks ago.

"His name is Bennie. Bennie . . ."

"Esposito," the boy said. He didn't offer to shake hands. I didn't either.

"I'm showing him around," AnnaLise said.

I frowned.

"I'm living with my aunt. My dad wanted me to stay with her and go to high school." The look on Bennie's face said he thought the idea was ridiculous.

"His father owns the carnival. Bennie has traveled all over the country," AnnaLise continued. "He's been to New York and Tennessee and Ohio and Florida." Her eyes grew wide. "The only place I've ever been was Chicago, but it was cold and dirty and I didn't like it very much."

I didn't say anything. I had never gone anywhere farther away than Bloomington.

"Hey, Andy. Can you do me a favor?" AnnaLise asked.

I nodded, not bothering to ask what it was. "Can you keep Bennie company for a few minutes? I have to go help with the box lunch." She wrinkled her nose. "I think it's a bunch of bunk, but my mom insisted." She leaned in close. I felt my breath quicken. "Mine's the one with horses on it."

Bennie watched her walk away. "She's very pretty," he said.

I nodded. "Yeah." I tried to think of something else to say.

"There's a basketball free-throw shooting contest later," I said. "Are you going to play?"

"What do you get if you win?" Bennie asked.

I had never been asked that question before. The free-throw contest had always been a part of life in Pierre. It felt strange trying to explain it to someone. "You get to say that you're the best free-throw shooter in Pierre, Indiana."

"Are there many people who try?"

"The whole town, practically."

Bennie cocked his head. "Maybe we can break our tie," he said.

I nodded. "But don't say—"

"I won't."

I grinned at him, glad we'd have the chance to finish our game.

Clarence Wannamaker, the fire chief, approached the table with the lunches. I licked my lips. "Gather 'round, men. It's time for lunch," he hollered.

A cheer went up from the crowd. I didn't say anything. I closed my hand around the money in my pocket and stared at the box with the pictures of horses. "All the proceeds go to the new fire truck," Chief Wannamaker continued. "So let's empty your pocketbooks and fill your bellies."

My heart pounded faster and faster the closer Mr. Wannamaker got to the box decorated with horses. He finally held it up. "What a pretty box," he declared. "And it feels heavy. I'd guess there's some pretty good eats in here. So what do you say, gentlemen, do I hear a dime?"

I flipped my hand in the air, trying to keep a low profile. "One dime from Andrew Soaring," the chief said. "How about two bits?"

Next to me, Bennie raised his hand.

I stared at him. He smiled. I pulled my money out of

my hand and counted it rapidly. "Four bits," I said. My voice croaked.

"Fifty cents from Andrew Soaring. Anyone else? Come on, gentlemen. Here's a chance on a mighty fine lunch."

"Fifty-five cents," Bennie said.

I counted again. "Fifty-nine." That was the last of my money. I nudged Bennie, hoping he'd take the hint and back down.

"One dollar," he said.

Chief Wannamaker whistled. "I have one dollar. Do I hear one twenty-five? He looked at me. I shook my head. "Then one dollar it is to the generous young man next to Andrew Soaring. Come on up here and meet your hostess."

I watched as Bennie strode forward to take the box. AnnaLise met him with a smile. I shoved my money back into my pocket.

Ham rushed toward me. "Hey, did you know you were bidding on my sister's lunch? Good thing you didn't win. Come sit with us and have some of Mom's chicken. Let's pity the poor fool who has to eat with AnnaLise. Who is it, anyway?" Ham stood up and stared at the pair. Then he turned to me with wide eyes, "Hey! Isn't that the kid—"

"Shh!" I demanded. Then I nodded. "It's him all right."

"No razzing? What's he doing here?"

I didn't feel up to telling Ham the whole story. "His name is Bennie," I said. I watched as Bennie and AnnaLise found a spot on the grass and sat down. A cold, hard knot settled in the pit of my stomach. I bit into a piece of Mrs. Mortimer's fried chicken, but it tasted like rubber in my mouth. I'll break our tie all right, I thought.

Chapter Twelve

"Petey? Petey!"

I had finished my lunch and was walking toward the limestone carvings. I wanted to see them, but mostly I wanted to get away from the sight of AnnaLise and Bennie. A thin, white hand plucked at my shirt.

I turned and saw Abigail Mortimer. She continued to pluck at my sleeve. "Mrs. Mortimer?" I tried to brush her hand away. "I'm Andy, Mrs. Mortimer."

"Don't worry, Petey," Mrs. Mortimer continued as if she hadn't heard me. "Claudia still loves you. She's just a young girl yet."

I felt tiny beads of sweat pop across my forehead. "I'm Andy, Mrs. Mortimer. Andy Soaring."

"I always knew the two of you were made for each other, Petey. Not like your dad and your mom. She married out of her league, if you don't mind my saying so. Of course, Claudette did, too, but she was such a pretty little thing.

And finding some nice boys from town to marry was your mother's idea. She's clever, that one. But listen to me." She fluttered her hand in front of her chest. "I'm gossiping like a schoolgirl."

"Ma'am?"

"And they did get married before you were born, that's the important thing, isn't it, Petey?"

"Mrs. Mortimer?" I took a step backward, but she followed me. I looked around wildly, hoping for someone to help me. "I'm Andy," I repeated. Mrs. Mortimer grabbed my arm. Her face as she peered into mine looked confused.

"Petey? Where's Petey? What happened to Petey?" Her voice rose to a wail. Tiny flecks of spittle foamed at the corners of her mouth. I stood paralyzed, rooted to the ground.

A figure broke from the crowd and strode toward us. "Mama. Mama, it's okay. Hush now, Mama." Felix Mortimer took his mother's arm and tried to steer her away. But she planted her feet and stared at him.

"Who are you?" she asked querulously. "Let go of me."

Sheriff Mortimer loosened his grip on his mother's arm, but kept hold. "It's Felix, Mama. Your son."

Mrs. Mortimer glared at him. "You're not Felix," she said. "Poor, poor Felix." She shook her head. "He might go to jail, you know."

"No, Mama," The sheriff said. He shook his head. "You're confused, Mama. I'm not *going* to jail. I *run* the jail. I'm the sheriff, Mama." He patted her shoulder. Behind us, several people murmured their sympathies.

Mrs. Mortimer blinked at him, her eyes red-rimmed and watery. "Will you escort me home, young man? My father will be angry if I'm out past nightfall. He says I'm too young to go courting."

Sheriff Mortimer extended a hand and bowed. "I would be honored to escort you home," he said. I took a deep breath, held it, and then expelled it slowly. The sheriff walked across the street with his tottering mother in tow. I shook my head, trying to clear it of Mrs. Mortimer's non-sense. She was crazy. Absolutely bonkers. What was she talking about? Questions niggled at the back of my mind. I felt as if I was staring at a blueprint for a building that was missing its cornerstone. I frowned, trying to sort it out. It was nothing, I decided. I turned and trotted toward the basketball goal. The free-throw contest would be start-ing soon. I could shoot some baskets and clear my head. If there was one place in my life where I knew what to expect, it was a basketball court.

The rules of the free-throw contest were simple. Everyone entered in the contest had to shoot three out of four free throws. Miss two shots and you're out. Make three and go to the next round. Then keep shooting until somebody misses. The year before I had come in second to Derrick Davidson, a senior on the basketball team who got married after high school and moved to Stinesville to work at his father-in-law's quarry. George had come in third. This year, I was the favorite, but George was a close second.

"Good luck, Andy," some of the townspeople shouted

as I took my place in line. I nodded in thanks, then I peered through the crowd, looking for my dad, but I didn't see him. I wondered where he was. I hoped he'd have a chance to watch. He had been so pleased, the time that Pete had won.

Bennie joined me in line. "You're not sweet on Anna-Lise, are you?" he asked.

"No!" I denied it emphatically, shaking my head. I didn't look at him when I spoke. "No! Of course not. She's my best friend's sister, that's all. I was only bidding so her feelings wouldn't get hurt."

Ham was watching from the sidelines. He waved.

"Her lunch was good," Bennie said. "I think her mother made it."

The chicken I'd eaten sat like a weight in my stomach. "It's time to play," I said.

"Good luck," Bennie said. I didn't answer.

The contest moved fast. There wasn't a lot of time to think. The referee, Mr. Malcolm, who was the grocer in real life, grabbed the ball and tossed it back the second a shot was made. The crowd cheered after each made shot and groaned with each miss. As I waited my turn, I saw Dad watching the contest and talking to some men from the mill. Ham was deep in conversation with a couple of the Baptist kids. I would have bet ten marbles he was working out some money-making scheme on the outcome of the contest.

When it was my turn I stepped to the free-throw line, took a deep breath, and quickly sank three shots in a row. After the last shot rolled cleanly through the net, I exhaled and closed my eyes. Nothing to worry about. I nodded at Bennie and George on my way back to the queue.

"All right! Way to go, Andy!" Ham hollered.

I joined the people who had also made their first three shots. Ham sauntered toward me.

"That's the way, Andy," Ham said in a low voice. "Those Baptist boys nearly lost their lunch when they saw how easy you made those shots. I tried to warn them, but you know how it goes. A fool and his money."

I gave Ham a worried look. "What do you mean?"

"Just this—you are looking at a rich man, buddy. You keep making those shots and leave the wheeling and dealing to me. You thought you made some bucks playing marbles, well, that's nothing."

"Are you betting on the free-throw contest?" I asked in a whisper. "Ham, gambling's illegal! You're going to get into trouble."

"It's just a friendly little wager."

"What if your dad finds out? What if the sheriff finds out?"

Ham rolled his eyes. "He won't care. Besides, he's not going to find out."

"How much did you bet?"

"Don't worry. I'll cut you in for ten percent. It's *your* shooting arm."

"How much? Two bits?"

Ham shook his head no.

"Four bits?"

"Well, not quite."

My eyes grew big. "Criminy, Ham, how much?"

"There's two-fifty in the pot, winner take all." Ham grinned.

"Two-fifty?" Several heads turned our way. I quickly lowered my voice. "Land sakes, Ham! That much?"

"'Course." Ham looked at me as if I had just failed the eighth-grade finishing exam. "You're a sure thing."

I swallowed the lump in my throat. Two dollars and fifty cents. But if I won, I'd get two bits. Twenty-five cents.

"Hey, look." Ham pointed. "It's that kid again. Bet he has a stomachache after eating with AnnaLise. What did you say his name was?"

"Bennie," I said. "Bennie something. His last name sounded Italian. Or gypsy, maybe." I had a strange taste in my mouth.

I watched Bennie walk toward the hoop for his turn. He moved like a cat, fluid and confident. He stepped to the line and shot the basketball. The ball sailed cleanly through the hoop. Ham whistled. "He's good," he said. "He's as good as you."

I frowned. "No, he's not. It's just that he gets a lot of practice, working at the carnival." The words were out of my mouth before I had time to bite them back.

"Who works at the carnival?" asked Bill Freelow, who was standing in front of me. Bill worked the channeler at one of the quarries. There were rumors that he ran moonshine in the winter, but Sheriff Mortimer had never caught him.

I pointed toward Bennie. "He does?" Bill asked. "Wait a minute. Is that the kid? The basketball-shooting kid?" Bill frowned. "Lost two dollars on that game and never made a shot."

Ham punched me in the arm. Then he walked back to the crowd.

"He uses a weighted ball," I said. "At least," I paused, "that's what I heard."

Bennie made his third shot. Bill muttered to himself until it was his turn. He walked to the line and shot, but his ball went nowhere near the basket. I saw Bill give Bennie a dark look as he stomped into the crowd.

I made it through round two and round three. The crowd got bigger and the number of contestants got smaller. I heard Ham working a deal to get some of the other boys to bet smaller amounts with larger odds. Once, I got distracted while I was shooting because AnnaLise hollered to her friend, and I thought she was talking to me. The ball hit the rim and wobbled for half a second before tottering in. I thought Ham was going to pass out. His face turned red before regaining its natural color.

More and more people missed their shots and moved out of the contest, but Bennie stayed directly behind me. I felt like I was in one of the Charlie Chaplin movies that played at the Warner. I shot three free throws, and then he shot three free throws. Neither one of us said a word. All we needed was someone offstage playing the piano.

"He's good," said Stilt Kline, who now stood in front of me. We watched Bennie sink three shots. Stilt was going to be a senior. He played center on the basketball team. Stilt stood six inches taller than me, so I had to look up to see his face. He was all arms and legs and he couldn't run and think at the same time, but none of that mattered because he was so tall that he was able to grab the jump ball after every basket. "Is he going to go out for the team this year?"

I hadn't even thought about that. "I don't know," I said. "Do you think the new coach would want him?"

"Why wouldn't he? He's a great shot."

Bennie sunk his last free throw. "But his dad owns that carnival that comes to town every August," I said.

Stilt watched Bennie walk back to the line with wide eyes. "No joshing? My dad hates that carnival." Stilt's dad was an outspoken teetotaler.

Stilt missed his next shot. I was surprised he'd made it that far. I made my next three. When I was walking back to the queue, someone grabbed my sleeve. "Hey, Andy. Is that kid really from the carnival?"

A group of faces studied me. "That's what I heard," I repeated. "I never went myself."

A buzz went through the crowd. Most of the people standing there were townsfolk—respectable, church-going people. The same people who sent around the petitions protesting the carnival.

Bennie hit his next three shots. This time the crowd didn't cheer, they mumbled.

"Down to the final round," Mr. Malcolm bellowed. "Four players left in the running. Each player takes three shots. You miss, you step out. Last shot to fall is the winner." The grocer grinned and clapped his hands together. "Stick around folks, we've got some fine young talent here. This could take a while."

"Go, Andy!" Ham hollered. A group of people cheered. The boys gathered around Ham had divided into a following. Nearly half were rooting for George, who was still in it, the other half for me, with a few left for Daniel Handkamp and a couple for Bennie—mostly girls.

I swallowed.

Mr. Malcolm leaned in close. "Let's have a good game, but don't take too long about it. The Ladies Auxiliary is setting out their pies, and I can smell a lemon meringue calling my name."

I nodded like I understood, but all of a sudden I was having trouble taking a deep breath and I couldn't smell anything. I looked at the crowd and saw Dad watching. He was talking with a group of men, and I could have sworn he was smiling. I *had* to win.

Daniel Handkamp went first. He was twenty-five years old and looked like he kept in shape by heaving limestone blocks with his bare hands. He didn't really have a neck to speak of, just a tiny head stuck on to a huge pair of shoulders. Daniel had never played organized basketball before, but that didn't really matter because everyone in Pierre knew how to shoot a free throw. He thought it was funny that he was up against three kids.

"Watch this, young pup," he told George as he gave him a nudge with his elbow. George nearly fell over.

"I guess Mr. Handkamp doesn't know the rule about seniors," I whispered.

"Shut, up, Andrew." George turned away from me and crossed his arms in front of him.

Daniel dribbled, took aim, and then launched the ball. The ball crashed against the backboard and dropped in. The hoop seemed to tremble. Daniel raised his arms in the air and the crowd cheered. His next shot went in much the same way. But his third shot hit the backboard with such force that it bounced backward over my head—I ducked—and hit Mr. Samson the blacksmith square in the gut. Mr. Samson doubled over. Daniel raced over to help him.

"Sure am sorry about that," Daniel said. "Guess I got carried away."

Mr. Samson nodded, still clutching his stomach. Mr. Malcolm retrieved the ball and tossed it to George. "Next!" he hollered.

George strode to the line. He took his time dribbling. George played basketball squarely by the rules. Coach said to dribble it a certain way, George dribbled. He stood the way he was supposed to stand and he threw the ball the way he was supposed to throw. Ham said George looked like he had the straight end of a hoe stuck up his back, but there was no denying that he could shoot a basketball. If he could manage to get himself into the correct position, he rarely missed. All three of his shots sailed cleanly through. Daniel Handkamp made himself a spot in the crowd, displacing several other people to do so.

"Not bad for a young pup," I said as I walked to the line.

I stared at the basket, forced it into my mind and everything else out, and shot. Three in a row. All clean.

Bennie walked past me to the line. A small smile played on his lips.

I felt shaky. I watched as Bennie's final shot sank through the net. He walked back to take his place behind me. "Still a tie," he said.

George made his next three shots.

I walked to the line. Calm down, I told myself. I could beat him easy. I dribbled and shot. Basket.

"Whoo-eee!" Ham hollered. "Do it again, Andy! Do it again."

Who did Bennie think he was, buying AnnaLise's box lunch? I asked myself. He didn't have any right to eat lunch with her. He barely even knew her. I dribbled and shot again. Another basket.

Behind me, I heard a commotion. I turned to look. Sheriff Mortimer, Bill Freelow, and Stilt Kline's father were elbowing their way through the crowd. They surrounded Bennie. George moved a step away.

"This is a fair and honest competition," the sheriff said. "We won't abide cheating."

"Sir?" Bennie said.

The sheriff nodded to Bill. "Check him. Make sure he doesn't have anything illegal."

Bill ran his hands over Bennie. Bennie stepped away and clenched his fists. "Hey!"

"What's the problem, Sheriff?" Mr. Malcolm asked.

"Just making sure our contest stays fair," the sheriff said. "I heard this kid is in the habit of using weighted balls." The sheriff looked at me. "Isn't that right?"

Mr. Malcolm shook his head. "There's no ball here but the one Andy's holding right now. Andy, you going to take your last shot or not?"

"Yes, sir," I said. I turned my attention to the basket and shot. The ball sailed through.

Mr. Malcolm grabbed the basketball. He checked it, and then the sheriff asked to check it. After a few moments of looking the ball over, the sheriff handed it to Bennie. Bennie had a strange look on his face as he walked toward the hoop. He dribbled the ball, but didn't catch it. The ball bounced twice and rolled across the ground. Bennie shook his head and walked away. I watched him go. The crowd murmured.

"Well, George," Mr. Malcolm called. "Looks like it's down to you and your brother. You still playing?"

"Yes, sir." George took the ball and shot three in a row.

My turn. I felt a sharp pang in my stomach, even though I told myself I hadn't done anything wrong. Bennie *had* played with a weighted basketball at the carnival. It wasn't my fault if other people found out about it. I walked to the basket. I tried to shake my mind clear, tried to focus on basketball. This was *my* game. Out of the corner of my eye I caught sight of my dad, watching. I took a deep breath and launched the ball. It rattled against the rim and then bounced, harmlessly, to the ground.

George whooped and jumped into the air. I blinked in disbelief. Then vaguely, as if from far away, I heard Ham's wail of anguish.

Chapter Thirteen

School started two weeks later, on September 17. It was Monday, wash day, and before school I had to haul water from the pump outside into the kitchen and then dump it into the reservoir on the stove where Mother boiled the clothes. I was glad I didn't have to stay to rock the cradle washer. It was easier than cleaning the clothes with a washboard, but it was still wet, tiring work. I changed into my school clothes, and then stared at George as he finished getting dressed.

"What are you wearing?" I asked. He had on a pair of Dad's old church pants. They were faded and slightly worn, but they were still obviously church pants. Mother had ironed a sharp crease down the middle.

"I'm getting dressed for school," he said. He adjusted his tie.

"In that? You look like a preacher."

George looked me up and down, his gaze resting on the patched knees of my knickers. "I look like a senior in high school," he said finally. "I'm not a little boy anymore."

I stuck out my tongue at his back as we thundered down the stairs toward the kitchen. Mother had packed our lunches in tin pails. "Please don't get dirty and don't scuff your shoes," she said. Some of the farm kids wouldn't start school until October, when the corn was shocked and shelled, but Mother insisted that we didn't live in a "holler" and we'd go to school like gentlemen.

"Have you heard anything about the new coach?" I asked Mother as I gathered my books and strapped them together.

"Just that the school board hired someone," she said. She took out a hunk of lye soap that we made last summer from wood ashes and lard. I liked to watch it suds up.

"Are you going to welcome him?" I asked. "Bake him a pie or something?"

"The school board will welcome him, I'm sure," Mother said. "Now go on. You'll be late." I trotted out of the house after George. "Straighten your tie, Andrew," she called.

"Want to catch the train, George?" I asked. If I timed it just right, sometimes I could run down the hill across the road from our farm and catch the 7:49 as it chugged toward Pierre. The depot was less than two blocks from school. It beat walking a mile and a half.

"You really shouldn't do that, Andy," George said. "It's kind of like stealing."

"Stealing?"

"You don't pay for the ride, after all." George raised his eyebrows and looked down his nose at me.

"Shoot. The stationmaster doesn't care. And the driver slows down if he knows I'm coming." But I decided to go ahead and walk. Not because George thought it was wrong, but because the men at the depot would razz me for coming in second at the free-throw contest. George hadn't said much about beating me, but he sure walked around like he owned the world since he'd won.

The grammar school and the high school were housed in the same building, a two-story brick and limestone structure with a new gym attached. A wide hallway with an entrance on both sides separated the six high school classrooms from the rest of the school. I met Ham by the high school entrance. We punched each other in the arm and acted like we weren't nervous. George and the other seniors leaned against the building and pretended to look bored.

"Hey, Ham!" AnnaLise ran across the schoolyard toward us. Her mahogany-colored hair streamed behind her. I forgot about punching Ham and concentrated instead on wiping the moisture from the palms of my hands. I felt a foolish grin spread across my face. I was working on a new carving, one that I thought I might give to AnnaLise someday. That would sure get her attention.

"You're not supposed to be here," Ham said. "You belong over there." He pointed to the other entrance. "With the other children. This area is for high schoolers *only.*"

AnnaLise ignored him. "Have you seen him?" she asked.

"Who?" Ham asked.

"You know." AnnaLise's eyes grew wide. Behind her, two girls giggled. AnnaLise took a step closer and said in a loud whisper, "Bennie. I want to introduce him to Netty and Sylvia."

I frowned.

"How should I know where he is?" Ham asked. "I haven't seen him since the picnic. He probably got so sick from eating your lunch that he up and died."

AnnaLise huffed. She turned to her friends. "Come on, we'll find him. Then you'll see how swank he is." She looked at me as she started to walk away. "Hi, Andy."

I stared at my shoes. The tips of my ears burned.

"So what's he like?" I heard one of the girls ask AnnaLise.

"He's swell," AnnaLise said.

"I heard he's just divine," the other girl said with another giggle. "Like Rudolph Valentino."

I wrinkled my nose.

"Don't be such a dingbat, Sylvia," Ham called after her. "Come on, Andy. Let's go." He rose to his feet, and we started toward the door to the high school wing.

"He doesn't look like Rudolph Valentino," I muttered. "He's just a dumb carnival kid."

"Yeah, a dumb carnival kid," said a voice behind me. A dark-haired boy clattered past me and grasped the handle of the door to the school. Then he turned.

"By the way, we're still tied." Bennie said before he disappeared into the school.

Chapter Fourteen

"Come on, Ham," I pleaded when school let out for the day. "Come with me."

"Aw, Andy," Ham said. "I want to go to the drugstore and buy the new *Whizbang*."

My mother didn't let me read that magazine. She said it was too racy. But that wasn't why I wanted Ham to come with me. "I'll only stay thirty minutes," I said. "I have to get home and do chores anyway. But I need you to rebound. Please." I couldn't wait to walk into the gymnasium as a high schooler and see what it felt like to shoot baskets in that grand space.

"Thirty minutes. That's all," Ham said.

I jumped, and then pulled him toward the gymnasium. Most of the building was deserted. Everyone was streaming out the doors at the other end of the school. From where I stood, I could hear the muffled echoes of their laughter and chatter.

We turned a corner past the cafeteria and opened another door, a newer door, with shiny brass hinges and a vaulted archway carved out of limestone. "Gymnasium," read the words etched on that stone. Next to it, in intricate detail, were carved a chisel and a mallet, tools of the stonecutter's trade. I pulled Ham through the doorway.

The smell of polished hardwood filled the air. I took a deep breath. The basketball court gleamed golden in the afternoon sunlight that splashed through the casement windows high up on the walls.

At the other entrance was a large bookcase, with the trophies and awards that the high school had won over the years. It held pictures of Pete and his sectional championship team. His picture was also in there as a memorial to those lost in the war. But I didn't want to look at them right now. I walked toward the basketball hoop.

"Stand under the basket," I told Ham. "Rebound for me."

I shot the ball and watched it fall through the net. Ham snagged it without moving his feet and tossed it back.

"I met the new coach the other day," Ham said.

I dropped the ball, but caught it on the way up. "You did? When? Why didn't you tell me?"

"I thought you'd want to meet him on your own," Ham said.

I shook my head. Sometimes he was so dense. I looked around the gymnasium. "Is he here?"

"I don't know. I don't think he starts officially until next week. The school board's paying him eighteen hundred dollars to coach basketball and track. He's going to teach physical training and geography, too."

I whistled. "What's he like?"

Ham shrugged. "Okay, I guess."

I wasn't getting any stories out of Ham about the new coach. But then, the new coach probably didn't have any of Ham's kind of stories. I changed the subject. "What's your sister doing this afternoon?" I asked. I bent my knees, eyed the basket, and shot.

"Which sister?" he asked. "Jenni and Marilyn are probably playing with paper dolls. That's all they do—"

"AnnaLise," I said quickly. Ham had five sisters. It would take all day if he told me about all of them. He tossed the ball back to me.

"Probably schooling Jalahar. She's nuts about that horse. But I don't guess she'll ever be able to ride him."

I didn't say anything. Just concentrated on shooting the ball.

"Claudia's talking about coming home for good," Ham said. "But I don't know why. She's lucky, living in a big city like that. Don't you think Chicago would be swell?"

I shrugged. "I dunno."

"You don't know? Think of it . . . music, dancing, speakeasies, and flappers." His eyes sparkled. He grabbed the ball and tossed it back. "Chicago's the place to be."

I launched the ball toward the basket and watched as it rattled in. "I heard it smells like a slaughterhouse." I shook my head. "And isn't there a lot of crime and corruption?"

Ham threw me the ball without moving any more than was necessary. "Aw, don't be such a wet blanket, Andy. You sound like George. No, you sound like my Uncle Felix."

"I do not." I scowled at him before turning my attention to the basket. I dribbled, refocused my attention, and shot.

Ham reached out an arm and caught the ball as it fell through the net. "Could you just move around a little?" I asked Ham. "At least *pretend* you're going to try to take the ball away from me."

Ham moved his feet, but his mind clearly wasn't in it. "I think AnnaLise is sweet on that boy Bennie," he said.

"She is?" I launched the ball, but it sailed wide of the basket. Ham groaned and shuffled to retrieve it. "Uncle Felix doesn't like him."

"Why not?"

Ham shrugged. "He doesn't like any of the Italians." He tossed the ball back to me. "For a while I thought Anna-Lise was sweet on you." He made a face.

"You did?" I pulled the ball close to my chest.

"Yeah. But she's not. Good thing, too," he said. "Remember how everyone acted when Pete started talking about getting married to Claudia? First Claudia smiled nonstop, and then she couldn't stop crying. Mom was the same way."

I shot the ball. It fell through the hoop. I didn't really remember much about it.

Ham tossed the ball to me. "Don't you think it's strange? All they talked about was getting married, but then Pete ran off to war and Claudia went to Chicago to work in that home for unwed mothers. . . ." Ham raised his eyebrows.

"It's an orphanage," I said slowly. This was something I never talked about. Not with anyone. Not even my best friend.

"Haven't you ever wondered?" Ham's eyes glittered like they did when he was telling a dirty story he'd heard from one of the inmates at the jail.

"Wondered what, Ham?" I asked. I clutched the ball tightly between my hands.

"Wondered if Pete and Claudia left town because Claudia was . . . you know . . ." he lowered his voice, "in the family way."

The ball left my hands and shot toward Ham's midsection like a missile. Ham fell to the ground with an *oof!* "Hey! What was that for?" Ham yelled. I ran toward him, but he grabbed my legs and brought me to the ground.

"Pete wouldn't do that!" I shouted, swinging wildly at his head. "You take it back!"

Ham rolled and tried to pin me. We grappled, throwing punches and sliding on the hardwood floor. "Ow! Stop it!" Ham hollered. "She's *my* sister. . . . I didn't mean . . ."

"Yes you did. Ow!" Ham threw a solid punch that connected with my right shoulder.

"I did not! Get off!"

I grabbed Ham's shoulders and rolled. I was determined to pin him and make him take back what he'd said, or what he'd nearly said, about Pete. But then someone grabbed me by my shirt collar and hauled me to my feet. I wiggled and lunged, but two large hands clasped my shoulders. "Lemme go!" I yelled as I tried to squirm away.

Ham crawled to his knees and then stood, staring at whomever had me captured. His face was red and splotchy, and a bruise was blossoming on his right cheekbone.

"Hello, Mr. Runyon. Sir," Ham said. His entire demeanor changed and his face wore a look of respect. I swiveled again to try and get a look at the man holding me.

"Hello, Harold. What seems to be the trouble here?" the man asked.

"Just having a little disagreement," Ham said. He looked at the floor. "It's nothing."

"Well, fighting's no way to solve anything, disagreement or not." The man finally released me. I was still mad at Ham, and now I turned to glare at the man who had pulled me off him. He was big and tall, with muscles nearly bursting his starched white shirt. He wore a hat pulled tight over thick, brown hair. A matted cord of scar tissue started under his chin and zigzagged its way toward his collar. I swallowed. He looked like somebody who could hold his own in a fight.

"How do you do?" the man said. "My name is Mr. Runyon." He held out his hand, grabbed mine, and then pumped it firmly.

"Andrew Soaring, sir." I glanced at Ham with the question in my eyes. Ham smirked and crossed his arms over his chest.

"Mr. Runyon is the new basketball coach," Ham said.

My mouth fell open in disbelief. I snapped it shut and tried to think what to say, tried to think of a way to explain. "Oh. Heck. I mean . . . Well, sir, Ham said that Pete . . . that my brother . . . well, he didn't say it, exactly, but he meant it. . . . I was just trying . . . that is . . ." I took a deep breath and stared at the ground. This wasn't working. "I . . . I'm sorry about the fight, sir."

Mr. Runyon looked me over. "Andrew Soaring," he said. "I hear you want to play basketball." His voice was low, but there was no doubt he was used to being obeyed.

"Yes, sir," I said.

"I hear you're a good shooter."

I lifted my head at that. "Yes, sir," I said again.

"Well, I don't tolerate fighting. Not on my team and not from my players."

I nodded weakly. "No, sir. It won't happen again."

"It had better not. There are other ways to solve our problems than resorting to violence." I stole a glance at his face and wondered how he had gotten that scar. I decided not to ask.

"You have a brother who plays basketball, too?" the coach asked.

"Yes, sir," I said. I sighed and decided to tell it all. He'd hear about George eventually anyway. "His name is George. He's a senior." I wondered if this coach was a stickler for playing seniors. I also wondered if he was going to be better or worse than Coach Crowley. So far it wasn't looking good.

"What year are you?" the coach asked.

I sighed again. "Freshman."

The coach nodded. "There are a couple of other freshmen who are interested in playing basketball. We may have enough boys for a junior and senior varsity team."

Junior varsity? I frowned. "What other freshmen?" I asked. I looked at Ham. "You going out for the team?"

Ham shook his head, eyes wide. "No way, not me," he said. "No offense, Coach."

"None taken," the coach replied.

"Jed Nelson?" I asked. "Does he want to play?" I'd known Jed Nelson all my life. He always *said* he wanted to play basketball, but he didn't like to run and he didn't like to practice. He'd quit before the first game.

"Yes. That name rings a bell. Then you. There's one more . . ." he said.

I knew without having to ask, but I forced myself to ask the question anyway. "Who is it?"

The coach took a notebook out of his jacket pocket and quickly flipped through it. "Bennie Esposito. Has a natural shot." Coach raised an eyebrow. "With all these shooters, we could have one great basketball team."

"Yes, sir," I said, but for the first time my heart wasn't in it.

Chapter Fifteen

The next three weeks flew by in a blur of schoolwork, corn harvesting, and brief stolen moments to practice shooting. The state declared that basketball season was allowed to begin October 1st, but Coach pushed it back to October 8th for those of us who had to help get the corn in. I had never shucked corn faster in my life. By the eighth it was cut, shocked, shucked, and loaded into the corncrib.

Ham told me that Bennie wasn't going out for the team after all.

"Why not?" I asked.

"Who knows? But I overheard Uncle Felix say that a carnival kid wasn't going to play basketball for Pierre. Said he didn't care how good he was, we didn't want that kind of person on the team."

I looked around, to make sure Bennie wasn't lurking nearby. I didn't see him. "The sheriff's probably right," I said.

"Aw, Andy. You're just sore because you never got a chance to beat him."

"That's not it." I just didn't like him very much.

Without Bennie, Jed Nelson and I were the only freshmen. Coach started us running and then put us to work on drills before we even got to practice shooting. Jed dropped out after the first hour. We didn't have enough players for a junior varsity team after all. I made the varsity lineup.

We practiced every day after school and on Saturday mornings. Our first game was at home on Friday, November 2, against Stinesville.

Excitement in the town reached a fever pitch. Storeowners hung green and gold banners in their shop windows. Farmers put green rosettes on their horse's manes when they drove into town. All day on Friday kids and teachers alike wished me luck.

I found myself face-to-face with Bennie before the last class of the day. "Will you play?" he asked.

I nodded. Coach said he was going to start George and me at forward, with Stilt at center, and Hale Brant and Theodore Crutcher at back guard.

Bennie made a strange face. "I've never played on a team. I've never even seen a real game. I just like to shoot."

There was an awkward pause. "Maybe we could shoot baskets sometime," I said.

Bennie grinned. "Yeah. I'd like that." He nodded, and then clapped me on the back. "Good luck tonight."

George and I rushed home after school. I fed the chickens, slopped the hogs, and cut a cord of wood for the fire. "Don't overdo it," Dad said.

I looked at him in surprise, and then grinned as I carried an armload of wood to the stove. "No, sir. I won't."

The air outside was crisp, but the stove warmed the house. Mother had dinner waiting—roast chicken, green beans, biscuits, pickled beets, and sweet potato pie. The gasoline lamps glowed cheerfully while we ate. There wasn't much talk during dinner. Everyone's mind was on the game. "I do enjoy basketball," Mother said suddenly as she cleared the table and put the dishes to soak.

Outside the daylight was fading. Two years before, the school board had voted to wire electricity into the school. Everyone said electric lights were cheaper and better in the long run. Mother and Dad agreed, but no one knew when the electric lines would be run out to the farms. Besides, I knew electricity cost too much, and Dad was still worried about the mortgage.

We piled into the Model T. This was my favorite time of year. The harvest was in and the cornfields were reduced to stubble. The trees on the hillsides blazed orange and red and gold. The work in the fields and in the quarries had slowed almost to a stop, and the air crackled with excitement.

I clenched my fists so tight that I made half-moon indentations on my palms.

The automobile rumbled toward town, joined by dozens of others. We had gotten some rain in October, but the roads were dry and still passable. In December Dad would put the car in the barn until spring, and we'd have to use the wagon.

George and I left Mother and Dad at the entrance to the gymnasium. We jogged toward the changing room. The school board had paid for our uniforms—white jersey, dark green padded shorts, dark green knee socks, and canvas basketball shoes. Mrs. McIntire, who ran the boarding house on Jacob Street, washed them for us before every game. My heart surged with pride as I pulled on the wool jersey with PHS embroidered in large green letters on the front.

"I think we're going to be good, really good," I said.

George nodded. "Just remember to listen to what Coach tells you."

I smiled at him. I had been to hundreds of basketball games in my life, but I had never played in one this exciting. Coach gave us our final instructions and then the reverend came in to pray. We walked into the gymnasium. Four rows of wooden bleachers encircled the court, and every seat was filled. Girls wore green and gold ribbons in their hair. A cheer went up from the crowd as we took our positions on the court. I scanned the faces and found Mother and Dad. They were both watching the court expectantly. Dad's face had lost that haggard and worn expression.

I saw Ham in the crowd. "Go, Andy!" he yelled. He was sitting next to his granna. She grinned and waved a green handkerchief. Ham had been sitting with her for an hour every day after school. He hadn't said much about it, but she looked like she was doing better. I waved, and then got ready.

The referee launched the ball into the air and another cheer went up from the crowd when Stilt tipped the ball to Hale Brandt. Hale quickly passed to Theodore, who dribbled up the court. I moved out of position to get away from my defender. Theodore passed me the ball, but the defender was too tight. I passed it to George, but he wasn't in position to shoot. He dribbled. I knew he wouldn't take the shot.

I cut across the court and shook off the Stinesville back guard who was tailing me. "George!" I called.

He frowned. "You're not in position," he shouted.

"I'm open! Pass."

George passed. I dribbled, eyed the basket, and shot. Goal!

The crowd burst into cheers.

I watched as Mr. Murphy changed the numbers on the scoreboard. Two to zero.

"Great job, Andy," Stilt said as he walked back to the center for the jump ball.

"Stay in position," George said as we got ready for the jump.

The Stinesville guard fouled me with eight minutes left in the first half. The score was six to two.

I heard the applause from the crowd as I trotted to the foul line. Both shots sailed cleanly through the basket. Eight to two. My first two foul points in my quest to beat Pete's record of eighty-eight free throws in a single season.

At halftime the score was sixteen to six. The crowd was on their feet, cheering and hollering as we took our break. As I left the court I saw Dad getting pats on the back from the men around him. Both his boys were starters, I thought proudly, and I was the leading scorer.

Coach told us how well we were playing. Told us not to slack off on defense because the Stinesville forwards could erupt at any moment.

"Great shooting, Andy," he said as we prepared to take to the court for the second half. "But watch your defense. You're leaving your man wide open."

"Yes, sir." The kid I was guarding couldn't hit the broad side of a barn.

"They don't know what to make of your left-handed set shot," Hale said as we trotted out to the court.

"Watch me this half," I said. "I'm going to take shots from so far back that Stinesville will think we got somebody shooting from outside the gymnasium."

"You're a real corker, Andy," Theodore said.

"Don't be a show off." George glared at me.

Stilt tipped the jump ball to me. I dribbled twice and then shot from behind the half-court line. The ball swished through the hoop. There was a moment of silence, and then a loud whoop filled the gym. The guard from Stinesville had his mouth open. Then he shook his head.

"You're going to wear me out, Andy," said Stilt as he prepared for another jump ball. "You keep scoring that way, I'll never get a break."

I grinned and raced down the court, ready for the next basket.

At the final horn we were ahead thirty-two to nineteen. I was the leading scorer with twenty points, eight of which were free throws. George had scored ten and Theodore two. As we left the gymnasium, Hale hoisted me onto his shoulders.

"Hurrah, Andy!" AnnaLise cheered as we passed. I smiled at her. She blew me a kiss, and I nearly fell off Hale's shoulders.

"Good game, boys." Mrs. Pickens, with a fountain pen and a sheaf of paper in her hands, met us at the locker-room door. "Read about yourselves in tomorrow's edition of the *Pierre Journal*. Tell me what you thought about the game."

No one spoke for a moment. Then I said, "Well, Mrs. Pickens, Stinesville had a good team, and they played hard, but they just weren't in the same class as your Pierre boys. They couldn't compete with our ability to put the leather through the hoop."

Mrs. Pickens scribbled on her paper. "Ability to put the leather through the hoop," she mumbled as she wrote. She looked up. "Very eloquent," she said. "From the Latin *eloquens*."

I felt myself flush. Hale Brandt punched me on the arm as we walked into the locker room to change out of our uniforms. "Eloquent," he said in a high, mocking voice. "Andrew is very eloquent."

"Good game, Andy," George said. "But when you're running around the court shooting from any old place, I can't set up Coach's defense."

"Aww, George." I buttoned my shirt and tucked it into

105

my knickers. I looked at him dressed in his church pants and I smiled. "Don't be such a boob."

The locker room exploded with laughter. Coach came in and told us how well we had played and said that now we had to calm down and get ready to play Martinsville the following week. Then we went to find our parents.

Mother and Dad were waiting by the gymnasium doors. They were both smiling. "Well done, George. Well done, Andy." Dad said. He patted my shoulder. "Great game."

Chapter Sixteen

The euphoria from our first win carried me through the weekend and into the following week's practice at school. The *Pierre Journal* printed an account of our win on the first page, mostly names and numbers, without the excitement of what had actually transpired, but my quote was in the story with Mrs. Pickens's observation that if "young Andrew Soaring continues to display such accuracy at the hoop, then the Pierre Carvers have a long and exciting season in store."

I felt so great that when I finished my carving I wrapped it in a page from the Sears, Roebuck catalog and left it on the Mortimers' front porch with a note. "To AnnaLise. From an admirer." The carving was of a horse grazing. Jeremiah Donegol from the mill said it was one of my best. After the kiss AnnaLise blew at the game, I figured she'd know it was from me.

On Wednesday, after practice, George and I changed

clothes and got ready to go home. As we left the school, I pretended to dribble a basketball. I danced around George, driving and shooting.

"Do you think Pete missed it?" I blurted after scoring an imaginary basket.

"Missed what? Would you settle down? Criminy, Andy."

"Missed playing basketball," I said. "When he was at war."

George shrugged. "He was probably too busy fighting the Germans to worry much about missing basketball."

I shook my head in disagreement. "No, I think he probably missed it. I mean, he practically invented basketball around here. I bet that between battles, when the soldiers had a break, he probably taught the other guys in his platoon to play. Maybe they even had games." I grinned, visualizing the scene in my head.

George snorted. "Sure, Andy. What do you think they used for a ball? Gunshot?"

I thumbed my nose at him. "I still wish I knew why he left," I said.

"Why he left what?"

"Why he left home. Why he left school. It was his senior year and Pierre was destined to go to the state tournament. We could have won it, too. Easily. And he had just turned seventeen years old. I mean, he had to lie about his age to even get into the army. Couldn't he have waited a year?" I didn't say what I thought—that if he'd waited a year he wouldn't have died.

George pursed his lips. I had stepped over the line. It wasn't something we talked about.

"Andy! Hey, Andy!" I turned around and saw Ham. I waved. Ham was standing at the crossroads of Homestead and Main streets. When he saw us he raced our way. "Hey!" Ham shouted. "You got to come see this! Bennie Esposito is riding AnnaLise's horse." His breath came in rapid gasps.

"AnnaLise's horse? Jalahar?" I asked. "What's *he* doing riding AnnaLise's horse?" My words sounded louder than I intended. Ham glanced at me.

"It started because Matthew Burke was teasing him, you know how he is, and asked him why he walked to school instead of riding a piebald pony like all the other gypsies. Bennie said that first of all he wasn't a gypsy, and second of all, who ever heard of a gypsy riding a piebald pony, and third of all, the horses around here were too humdrum for him, anyway. Then AnnaLise said he should ride Jalahar. She said that anybody who could carve horses the way he can ought to be able to ride them." Ham waved his hands expressively. I could feel my jaw muscles start to throb.

"Anybody who could carve horses . . . ?" I felt like I'd been kicked in the gut.

"Bennie left a present for her on our front step. Boy, was Uncle Felix mad!"

My mouth gaped open. I tried to find the words to explain that the carving had been from me, but my tongue felt numb.

I started walking in the direction from which Ham had come. Ham jogged to keep up.

"Where are you going?" George called.

"I'm going to see this." I took long, loping strides. I felt like I was marching into battle.

"You've got chores! And Mother will have supper ready."

"It will only take a minute."

George made a noise in the back of his throat, but then he trotted after us.

"So, what happened?" I asked Ham.

"Well, first Bennie went home. We waited awhile for him to come back. Everybody thought he was going to chicken out, but he didn't. He turned up at the corral wearing this shiny, red, circus-looking outfit. I thought AnnaLise and her friends were going to bust."

"Bust?"

"Oh, you know how they get. They practically swoon every time Bennie opens his mouth. And when they saw what he was wearing, well, you'd have thought he was some kind of movie star."

I scowled. "Red circus pants? I bet he looked ridiculous."

"You would think so, but he didn't. He's a real corker," Ham said.

"So then what?" I asked.

"Then AnnaLise brought out Jalahar. He hadn't been for a run in a couple of days, so he was kind of wild-eyed. His ears were laid back like he'd as soon take a bite out of you than anything. I think AnnaLise knew Jalahar would be out of control."

I chuckled. "So did he get scared?"

"No. Here's the strange part. Bennie walked right up to Jalahar, put his hands on his neck, and started mumbling."

Ham shook his head. "It was just like that time at the carn—" I punched Ham in the shoulder. His eyes widened and he glanced at George. There was an awkward pause, but luckily George seemed oblivious.

"So what did he say?" I asked Ham.

"Who?"

"Bennie. What did he say to the horse?" It sounded like madness to me, talking to a half-crazed horse. Everyone must have thought he'd lost his marbles.

Ham shrugged. "I don't know what he said. It sounded like a lot of jibberish. But Jalahar calmed right down."

"What did AnnaLise do?" I asked. I had a nasty taste at the back of my throat, like I had just been given a dose of cod-liver oil.

"She couldn't believe it. She asked him what he did. He just smiled and asked was she ready to see him ride." Ham's hands were going full speed, as if he could draw the scene in front of him if he waved hard enough. I didn't need him to sketch it for me. The pictures of AnnaLise and Bennie smiling at each other over the back of her stallion, came unwanted into my mind.

"Aw, anybody could ride that horse," I muttered. "Once he's out of the stall and settled." I tried not to think about actually *getting* that horse settled.

Ham grinned. "I knew it. I knew you'd say that. I said the same thing to AnnaLise. I told her that you could ride Jalahar, too, no problem. She said you didn't like horses." Ham chuckled and shook his head. "What do girls know, anyway?"

I came to a dead stop. Ham and George walked a few steps farther, and then slowed and looked back at me. "Are you coming?" Ham asked.

"You told AnnaLise that I could ride Jalahar?" I asked in disbelief. "Why . . . why did you tell her that?"

Ham shrugged. He looked decidedly unconcerned. You can, can't you? I mean, you have horses."

George raised one eyebrow. The corners of his mouth twisted into a funny smile. I decided not to look at him. "Of course I have horses." I gazed up. Gray clouds scuttled on a chill wind. "And I can ride them, too. If I want."

"That's what I said. So come on." Ham started walking.

"Where?" I asked. I trotted to catch up.

"To watch you ride Jalahar. I've got two dollars on it."

"You're gambling?" George's lips pinched together in a disapproving line. "Ham! You ought to know better."

Ham laughed. "Don't be such a stick-in-the-mud, George. Besides, I have to make up my losses."

That clinched it. George didn't know about the money Ham had lost because of my missed shot during the free-throw contest. And I didn't want him to find out.

"I'll do it," I said. "I'll ride Jalahar. It'll be easy."

"Andy! You can't ride that horse." George leaned close. "And you certainly shouldn't be gambling."

"I'm not gambling," I said. "All I'm going to do is ride a stupid horse."

George was quiet for a moment, but then he shook his head and followed us.

A group of kids clustered around the corral gate. They broke into a cheer as we walked toward them. In the middle of the corral, Jalahar snorted and pawed the ground. I wiped my hands on my pants. I glanced at the horse and then whispered to Ham, "I thought you said Bennie got him settled."

"He did." Ham shrugged. "But then he rode him. I guess being ridden got him all worked up again."

AnnaLise broke away from the crowd and walked toward me. I tried to smile at her, but my face felt stiff. I couldn't even blink.

"Ham says you're going to ride Jalahar," she said. She put her hands on her hips and cocked her head. I wondered if my entire body had turned to stone.

"Er . . ." My voice squeaked, so I paused and tried again. "Sure. Sure I am."

She stared at me. Oh, please, I thought. Please don't let me do anything dumb.

"You don't have to, you know," she said. "Ham's just trying to make some easy money."

Out of the corner of my eye I saw Bennie leaning against the railing of the corral. The sun caught the sequins on his outfit, making him flash and sparkle. Two of the girls from AnnaLise's class stood a few steps away.

"I want to," I said loudly. "It's easy. Anybody could do it." I took several long, fast steps to the corral before I could talk myself out of it. It really wasn't a big deal, I thought. I wasn't scared.

"Okay, everyone, we've already seen Bennie ride the horse. He stayed on for about twenty seconds, wouldn't you say?" Ham asked. The crowd nodded. "Twenty-four seconds," someone said. "I used my dad's pocket watch."

Ham nodded. "So that's what Andy has to do. Twenty-four seconds on the back of Jalahar. William, you count on your dad's watch again. Ready, Andy?"

I took a deep breath. Twenty-four seconds wasn't very long, I told myself. I released my breath with a loud whoosh.

"Ready," I said.

"Okay, then. Let's go."

I nodded. Someone opened the gate, and I walked into the corral. I felt like I was in a trance.

Jalahar pawed the dirt. I clucked softly and tried to remember what Bennie had done to calm him that night at the carnival. I hadn't wanted to go near Jalahar that night, either, I remembered. But that wasn't because I had been *scared*. And I wasn't scared now. After all, I reminded myself, Abigail Mortimer had ridden him. If she could ride him, then I certainly could. I took a deep breath and made another clucking noise. Jalahar flicked his ears.

"Ham, this isn't a good idea," AnnaLise said. "I don't want him to get hurt."

I looked toward the gate where AnnaLise stood watching. "It's okay," I said. "I won't get hurt."

"Not you, Jalahar. Hey, watch out!" AnnaLise said.

I wheeled around to see Jalahar's head snaking toward me. I jerked to the side as his teeth snapped, barely missing my arm.

"Jalahar's not used to just anybody," AnnaLise said. "What if he tries to buck with a rider on his back? If my horse gets injured, Ham, I'm holding you responsible."

My warm feelings vanished, replaced by a knot of fury.

"That's it," I muttered to the horse. "You horrid, murderous bag of oats. I am going to ride you if it kills me."

I stalked up to the animal and grabbed the halter. Jalahar tried to whip his head around again, but I held the halter too tight. Before I could think about what I was doing, I put my foot in the stirrup and launched myself into the saddle.

For a moment, Jalahar stood frozen. I gathered the reins and grinned. Twenty-four seconds. This was going to be easy. It wasn't like I had never ridden before. I had horses— two of them. They were draft horses, not thoroughbreds like Jalahar, but they were still horses. I leaned forward and tapped Jalahar on the withers to move him into a walk.

Jalahar exploded. He launched himself skyward and then sideways. I grabbed for his mane, trying to wrap my arms around the coarse hair, but Jalahar thrust his head down and twisted. I was torn loose from the saddle and catapulted into the air.

The world spun in a blur of browns, blues, and grays. I didn't know where I was until I hit the ground with a sickening thud. A shock of pain rocketed down my left arm and everything turned black.

From what seemed like far away I heard screams and voices and the pounding of footsteps. Gradually the voices came closer. I tried to open my eyes, but I couldn't see.

"He's dead, isn't he? Oh merciful God, he's dead!" It was the voice of one of AnnaLise's friends. Someone started to scream.

"Be quiet, Netty. He's not dead." That was AnnaLise. "Are you, Andy? Are you dead?"

I tried to open my mouth, tried to tell her that I didn't think I was dead, but I couldn't get my voice to work.

"Ham! Go and get the doctor. Quick!" That was George. He would tattle. I wondered what Dad would do to me as punishment.

I must have fallen asleep because when I opened my eyes, faces swam in front of me. There was George and Ham and AnnaLise and Doctor McNamara. "I'm not dead," I muttered. My voice sounded cracked. I tried to wet my lips with my tongue.

Their faces looked worried. "Of course you're not dead," Dr. McNamara said. "We're just going to get you loaded into my wagon, and I'll take you to my office so we can set that arm of yours."

I tried to ask what was wrong with my arm, but the pain that had lodged in my shoulder ricocheted into my back and legs. I closed my eyes.

"Don't you worry now," the doctor said. "You're young and strong. You'll mend in no time."

I felt hands grab me and hoist me into the back of Dr. McNamara's wagon. A searing pain exploded across my chest.

When I opened my eyes again, I saw Ham's face peering anxiously into mine.

"Doc say's you'll be okay," he said. He chewed his lips.

"How many seconds?" I asked.

"Hunh?" Ham looked confused. "Oh," he said finally. "Six."

"Six?" I blinked. "That's all? Six?"

Ham nodded.

I cleared my throat. "I'm . . . I'm sorry," I said. "I don't know what happened. I didn't mean for you to lose more money."

"It's okay." Ham reached out and patted me on the opposite shoulder, the one that didn't throb with pain. "I didn't lose any money."

"But I thought . . ." I wasn't sure what I wanted to say. Everything seemed to muddle in my head.

Ham looked apologetic. "I put my bet on Bennie."

Chapter Seventeen

The doctor wrapped my arm in cotton batting, and then covered it with plaster-of-paris-soaked gauze until it was entombed from fingertips to armpit.

"The plaster of paris will harden and prevent the broken bones in your arm from moving," he said. "The weight of the cast will keep the break in your collarbone from over-lapping and knitting incorrectly. I'll make a sling for you, which will take some of the weight. The break in your humerus"—he pointed to the top part of my arm—"looks pretty bad, but I think it'll heal nicely. Let's hope there's no infection. You're lucky you weren't hurt worse. The Judge is out of his mind letting his little girl keep that horse."

I stared at my left arm—white, solid, and immobile. I tried to find my voice. "How long will this be on?" I asked finally.

"At least two months."

"Two months?" My head jerked upward. I looked at the

doctor and then at my dad, who hadn't said a word during the entire process. "Two months? That's half the season!" The sudden movement hurt. I winced. "I can't play like this," I said.

"It takes time to heal." The doctor shrugged. "If those bones don't have the chance to knit together like they're supposed to, your arm will grow unevenly."

I stared at him in horror.

"If the bones heal correctly, by next year you should be as good as new."

"Next year?"

"Good thing he's only a freshman, eh, Henry?" The doctor helped me to my feet. "We've got three more years of games like last Friday night's to look forward to."

Dad just nodded and escorted me to the car.

"You could have been killed," was all he said during the long, jolting ride home.

I missed the game against Martinsville on Friday night. Mother wouldn't let me leave my bed. She said I needed rest, but the throbbing pain in my shoulder kept me from sleeping. Dad said there was nothing the doctor could give me for the pain except morphine. I lied and said it didn't hurt.

I heard the family come home after the game. I listened as they stomped around downstairs. "What happened?" I asked when George finally came up to our room.

He looked me over, from my head to the tip of my solid, white cast. "You are so selfish," he said. "You were too busy showing off to think about anybody else." That was all he said, and he refused to talk to me the rest of the night.

I read about the game in Saturday's *Pierre Journal*. "Local Boys Fall," announced the headline. "The Pierre boys lost in their gym 32 to 14. George Soaring was the top scorer with 10 points. Hale Brandt contributed 2 and Barry 'Stilt' Kline 2. Our boys will travel to Ellettsville next Friday, and then have a break until November 30, when they will return to the Carvers gym and take on Vincennes. Forward Andrew Soaring suffered a broken arm and collarbone this Wednesday last, and will be unable to play until January, according to our own Doctor McNamara."

I tossed the paper aside. But what happened? I fumed. I tried to imagine the game. How many shots did we get off? How many did we miss? What about our defense? Who scored for Martinsville, and why did we let them score? Did Stilt get the jump balls? Why'd we only score fourteen?

Mother kept me home the following week from school. Dad hired one of the neighbor boys to help with the milking. He and George couldn't manage it alone, and I was helpless.

Ham visited, bringing my schoolbooks with a couple of magazines snuck in. AnnaLise brought cookies, but she stayed in the living room and I stayed in my room, so I didn't see her. I didn't want to see her. Coach Runyon stopped by, too, but I pretended to be sleeping.

By Thursday I thought I was going to die of boredom. After George left for school I got up, clumsily wrapped a blanket around my nightshirt, and crept downstairs to the living room. Mother and Dad were talking in the kitchen and didn't hear me.

"I'll have to sell the tractor," Dad was saying.

"But what about next year's plowing and seeding? How will you manage without the Whitney?"

I frowned and leaned forward on the sofa, trying to hear.

"I could take a job at the mill."

"Henry . . ."

"If I don't do something to pay the note on the mortgage, we'll lose the land and the house."

"We should never have taken that loan out with Felix," Mother said. "I'm sorry. I thought the new farm equipment would be such a benefit. I thought that Felix would . . . because we've always been such friends. . . ." Mother's voice choked.

Dad cleared his throat. "He's a businessman, Beatrice. And he *is* renting the land that borders the Vigo Quarry." A chair creaked and I heard heavy footsteps walk through the kitchen toward the living room. I leaned back on the sofa and closed my eyes.

"Andrew?"

"Oh. Dad." I didn't know what to say.

He looked me over. "Take care of that arm," he said. His face looked so sad that it made me ache. He walked out the front door and stomped toward the barn. A few minutes later I saw him park the tractor in the yard, under my basketball hoop. He took a rag out of his pocket and began to clean the tractor.

On Friday night Pierre lost to Ellettsville twenty-nine to twenty-one. Dad told me the score. George still wasn't speaking to me.

Saturday morning, Mrs. Mabel Pickens came to call, clutching the latest edition of the *Pierre Journal*. I heard Mother open the door. Then, with a bemused look on her face, she escorted Mrs. Pickens into the living room.

Mrs. Pickens was wearing a dress, a silk dress with yellow polka dots, paired with a wool pullover sweater and a fur wrap. She gracefully removed the wrap and handed it to Mother. Mother carried it gingerly to the cedar chest and placed it inside. Mrs. Pickens walked toward me with the newspaper, and I noticed that she was wearing boots. Thick-soled men's boots. She handed me the newspaper and then turned to sit in a chair across the room.

"Such a lovely fireplace," Mrs. Pickens said, settling herself by the room's only source of heat. We didn't normally use the living room in the winter, preferring to huddle in the warmth of the kitchen, but there wasn't anywhere in the kitchen for me to rest.

"Thank you," Mother said. "Would you like some tea?"

"That would be lovely. Thank you, Beatrice," Mrs. Pickens said.

She didn't look like she talked, I decided after studying her for a few minutes. She talked like she was going to a fancy dinner party. She dressed like she had fallen into Mother's Christmas donation box of clothes for the needy.

While she and Mother sipped tea and made uncomfortable small talk, I scanned the newspaper for a story about the basketball team. There was a story, but it didn't tell me any more than I had already learned from George. We'd lost. Period. The end.

"I would like to hire young Andrew," Mrs. Pickens said

abruptly, catching my attention. "I need a correspondent."

I blinked and looked at Mother. She looked as perplexed as I felt. "A correspondent?" I asked.

Mrs. Pickens nodded.

"Andrew can't deliver newspapers," Mother said. Her eyebrows drew together in concern. "He has a broken arm."

I thought the fact was blatantly obvious.

"I don't want him to deliver the newspaper," Mrs. Pickens said. "I would like him to write for the newspaper."

Mother and I both stared at her as if she'd just asked me to run for mayor.

"I understand that you shoot the basketball with your left hand, which is currently mending?" Mrs. Pickens asked.

"Yes, ma'am."

"But you write using your right hand?"

I nodded, feeling more bewildered by the moment.

"Thus you are ambidextrous. Latin *ambi*—on both sides and *dexter*—right-handed."

"Andrew can't write for the newspaper," Mother said.

"He most certainly can. Several people in the community have"—Mrs. Pickens paused—"suggested that I expand the basketball coverage in the *Pierre Journal*. I myself know little about basketball. Therefore, I must find a correspondent who has a strong knowledge of the game as well as an ability to discuss said knowledge. Andrew came immediately to mind."

"Me?" I asked. I still wasn't clear what she wanted me to do. "You want me to write about basketball?" I shook my head. I was a basketball player, not a writer.

"As you know the *Journal* publishes on Wednesday and

Saturday," Mrs. Pickens said. "I would need a story about the upcoming game by Tuesday afternoon, and another story about the game immediately after it ends on Friday night. I hold a space in the paper for game coverage, but there isn't much time to get the type set before we have to go to print. There is also a certain word limit that must be met."

There was another long pause as Mother and I stared at the newspaper editor.

"I will pay him a small fee per story," said Mrs. Pickens. Mother cocked her head. "Oh," she said. "Oh!"

"He may start this week," Mrs. Pickens declared. "I would like an article on Tuesday. As there is no game this coming Friday night, he may write about how the team plans to spend this break regrouping after Andrew's—after his—injury."

I opened my mouth to protest, to say something, about the ridiculousness of this idea.

I was interrupted by heavy footsteps pounding up the front steps. The door burst open. Dad rushed into the room. Mother and Mrs. Pickens both stood up looking alarmed.

Dad's hair stuck out from his head at wild angles, and his breath came in rapid, shallow bursts. "Beatrice!" he hollered. "Telephone Sheriff Mortimer!"

Mother moved toward the phone without question. "Whatever in the world . . . ?" Mrs. Pickens asked. I saw her pick up her pad of paper and pull a charcoal pencil from behind her ear.

"The tractor!" Dad said. "It's been stolen!"

Chapter Eighteen

"Stolen?" Mrs. Pickens repeated. "Are you quite sure, Henry?" Her pencil hovered over the paper.

"Am I sure?" Dad raised his eyebrows and his face grew red. "I was mending a harness in the barn when I heard a terrific noise. I rushed out just in time to see my tractor being driven away by someone wearing goggles."

"A bootlegger?" I imagined the excitement that would cause if our tractor had been stolen to haul moonshine.

"Heavens," Mother said, looking at me as she talked on the phone. I wondered how many people were listening in on the line. By this afternoon everyone would know our tractor had been stolen.

"Preposterous," Mrs. Pickens declared. But she jotted something on her notepad.

Dad sagged against the doorframe. "That tractor . . . it's the only thing . . ."

I looked at Mrs. Pickens to see if she was still writing, but she clapped her hands together, causing me to jump. "Now, let's not panic. Whoever it was can't have gone far. Has anyone considered that the tractor thief might be George? Perhaps it's a prank?"

I shook my head. George didn't play pranks. As if to prove my point George ran up the walk and into the house. "The Whitney . . ." he hollered.

"We know," Mrs. Pickens said. "But whoever took it can't have gone far."

Mother finished talking and hung up the telephone with a loud clang. We all followed Mrs. Pickens outside. "Look," she pointed. On the other side of the barn, on a stretch of dirt that divided two fields, we saw a plume of exhaust.

"The tractor!" Dad said. He started running. Mother, Mrs. Pickens, and George raced after him. I held the weight of my cast with my right arm and hobbled as quickly as I could. The chickens that were scratching in the front yard flapped out of our way.

Once we reached the barn we could see the tractor. Whoever had stolen it was driving in wild jerks. We started to run toward it, but another car drove into the yard and stopped in front of us with a grinding screech of brakes.

"It's the sheriff!" I yelled as I caught up.

Sheriff Mortimer and Ham jumped out of the Packard. Everyone started talking.

"The tractor's been stolen," Dad said.

"Do you think it's bootleggers?" I asked.

"My granna's missing," Ham yelled.

126

We all looked toward the black-coated figure on the tractor. "You don't suppose . . ." Mother began.

"No way to tell until we get closer," Mrs. Pickens said. "Let's go!"

As we ran to the field, the tractor turned and rumbled straight at us. "Out of my way!" the figure yelled. The driver was wearing a large black overcoat with a white scarf and a pair of driving goggles. A broomstick bobbed alongside. "I'll gun you down!"

"That's my tractor!" Dad hollered.

"It's Granna!" Ham yelled. He jumped up and down and waved his arms. "Granna! Granna! Stop!"

"She's going to run us over," Mrs. Pickens observed in a voice much calmer than I felt. I half-expected her to take a notebook out of her pocket and begin jotting notes about our impending demise. We all began waving our arms and shouting for Mrs. Mortimer to stop.

The front end of the tractor roared to a halt just a few inches from where Ham was standing. He let out his breath and leaned against it. "Granna!" he said again.

"You're friendly?" Mrs. Mortimer asked. She stood up and motioned us toward her. "Well, then, grab your guns and climb aboard." She patted the seat of the tractor.

"Mama? Calm down, now. This is Henry Soaring's tractor. You're at his farm, Mama," Felix said. He looked apologetic as he turned to Father. "We took her to Warner's Theater last week. They ran war footage before the feature. She must have gotten the movie confused with . . . well, with real life."

Dad looked with wide, disbelieving eyes from Felix back to Mrs. Mortimer.

"Henry Soaring? He doesn't need a tractor. He's a quarryman, the one who married that drunkard's daughter from the holler." Mrs. Mortimer shouted. She looked from face to face but didn't show any recognition. "Where is he? He'll want to come. Because it's Petey we're after, Petey Soaring! He's been captured by the Germans."

Mother gasped. Her face grew white. Mrs. Pickens cocked her head and studied Mother. "Are you all right, dear?" she asked.

"Yes, yes," Mother said softly.

"Granna, come on down now," Ham said. "It's time to go home. You can't rescue anyone."

"I tell you I can!" Mrs. Mortimer bent down and picked up the broomstick that was lying on the runners. She pointed the end of it at us. "I don't want to use this, but I will if I have to. Now get out of my way. I'm going to get Petey come hell or high water. He's a Pierre boy and those Germans can't have him."

"Granna!" Ham wailed. He looked at me in desperation.

Mrs. Mortimer peered down at him. "Who are you?" she asked.

Ham's face fell. "Granna! I'm Ham!"

"Mrs. Mortimer?" I said. I cradled my broken arm and shuffled toward her. "Pete's . . . Pete's dead, Mrs. Mortimer."

Mrs. Mortimer blinked. I could feel everyone's eyes on me.

"Petey?" Mrs. Mortimer asked. "Is that you?"

"No, Mrs. Mortimer," I said. "I'm . . ." Then I looked into her frightened face. "I mean, yes. Yes, it's me. Petey."

I heard my mother catch her breath. "What in the—" Felix began, but Mrs. Pickens grabbed his arm and he stopped.

"What happened to your arm, Petey?" Mrs. Mortimer asked.

I looked at my enormous white cast. "I hurt it in the war," I said.

"I always liked you, Pete," Mrs. Mortimer said. "You're a good boy. It never mattered to me one bit that you were an early baby." Mrs. Mortimer chuckled. "Now that you're home you can marry."

"Yes, ma'am. But maybe you best go home now, ma'am." She looked around blankly for a moment, but then she handed me the broomstick and allowed Felix to lead her toward the car. Ham followed. He looked back once, staring at me with a puzzled expression. I shrugged.

"Well done, Andrew," Mrs. Pickens said once they had all piled into Felix's Packard. "You are quite the dramatist."

I felt heat rush to my face.

"She's a menace," declared Mother. Her face was a ghostly white. "They ought to keep her locked up! Coming into our home with her innuendos . . ."

Mrs. Pickens studied Mother. "Don't fret, dear," she said. "She will have forgotten this whole incident by the time she gets home."

Sheriff Mortimer started his car. After it sputtered to life, he walked back to us. "Sorry," he said over the roar of his engine. I saw Ham and Mrs. Mortimer encased in the back seat. "She's got this war nonsense in her head. To-morrow it will be something else." Felix shook his head, walked back to the car, and climbed into the driver's seat. We stood in silence and watched the car drive away.

Mrs. Pickens clapped her hands. "Well, all's well that ends well," she said. "Your tractor is back, safe and sound. No one got injured or hurt in any way. You can put this whole experience behind you."

Dad nodded. He walked toward the tractor and patted it on the fender. "Who would have even guessed she knew how to get this old thing started?" he said incredulously to no one in particular. "Or drive it?"

Mother shook her head. George looked confused. "I don't understand."

I spun the broomstick in my good hand. "She was going to rescue Pete. Bring him home."

The rest of my family looked at me as if I were the one who was crazy. Then they all went back to what they were doing. I stayed outside with the broomstick, wondering if maybe Mrs. Mortimer was the only one who made any sense.

Chapter Nineteen

I went back to school on Monday. Some of the smaller boys stopped their game of marbles and stared as I passed. The older boys greeted me in the school yard. "Hey, Andy!" called Hale Brandt. "Good to see you back." He whistled at the sight of my arm. "I heard it was your shooting arm." He shook his head sadly. "So what really happened? There've been rumors . . ."

"Rumors?"

Hale shrugged. "You haven't heard? Regular stuff, you know. Something was wrong with the horse, or you and Ham had some kind of scheme that went bad . . ."

"Something *was* wrong with the horse," I said quickly and without thinking about what I meant.

Hale leaned in close. "Really? What?"

I thought back to the day. Bennie, dressed in that fool costume; Jalahar, wild-eyed and crazy. "Bennie did something to Jalahar," I said, forcing myself to believe the words to be true as soon as I spoke them. Why else would the horse have acted the way it did? "He fixed it, just like he fixed the contest at the carnival," I continued, thinking out loud.

Hale nodded, looking grave. "Geez, Andy. I bet you're right." He shook his head. "Stupid carnival kid. He cost us our best player."

I watched Hale stomp away, feeling only a slight twinge of guilt about the rumor I'd just started. But maybe it wasn't a rumor. Maybe it was true.

"Hi, Andy." I turned at the sound of AnnaLise's voice.

"Hi, AnnaLise," I stared at her. "Wow. What'd you do to your hair?"

All her long, mahogany hair was gone, cut to just below her ears. "I got a bob," she said. She shook her head, swishing her short cap of dark hair. "Do you like it?"

"Yeah," I said. "I mean, sure."

She smiled at me. Then she looked at my arm and frowned. "I sure am sorry about your arm. Does it hurt something awful?"

"No. It just itches a little." I didn't tell her that sometimes I woke up in tears in the night because it itched and burned so fiercely.

"The Judge sold Jalahar."

"He did?" I paused. "I sure am sorry." I tried to think of a way to tell AnnaLise that the carving left on her doorstep had been from me, but I couldn't get the words out.

"It's okay. A man in Kentucky bought him. He's going to race him." AnnaLise shrugged. "Maybe he'll be a champion."

"Oh." I didn't know what to say to that. "Hey, um, you know that carving . . . ?" But AnnaLise wasn't listening. She waved and walked toward the junior high entrance. A large figure loomed behind me.

"We've missed you, Andrew," said Coach Runyon.

"Thank you, sir," I said. I couldn't quite meet his eyes.

"Are you feeling better? I tried to visit, but your mother said you were resting."

"Yes, sir. I'm feeling fine." I lied.

"I heard that you're going to start covering basketball for the *Pierre Journal*." I nodded. "I want you to know that I'll be happy to help you in any way I can."

"What are you going to do without me?" I blurted. "I mean, how will you win?"

Coach laughed. I flushed. I hadn't meant to sound arrogant, but no one else on the team could score twenty points a game. "You are surely missed," Coach said. "We aren't the same team without your net sniping ability." I smiled. Net sniping ability. I liked the way that sounded. "The other boys on the team will have to play above their best until that cast comes off and you're back to your old form. But I think we'll do okay. We still have a chance at the state tournament."

I nodded. Coach patted me on the back and walked toward the school. The cast would come off in January. The tournament started in March. I stared at my arm. Would it be ready? I wondered. Would the bones heal?

After school I wrapped my books with a strap and carried them with my right hand. George stayed for basketball practice. I didn't want to watch, so I walked home, stopping first at the mill.

The familiar sound of water grating on gravel assaulted my ears. The mill wasn't working at full capacity since the quarries had shut for the winter, but they still had a number of men cutting and planing and carving stone for market. The air was thick with limestone dust and the workers were covered with a soft, gray powder.

"Good to see you, Andy," Gene hollered. "You haven't been around in a while. Got more stone going to Washington, D.C., over here."

I nodded. He walked toward me. "How's your dad?" he asked.

"Fine."

"Good. You tell him I'll get somebody to get out to your farm and drill some cores as soon as the weather warms up." He directed his attention to my arm. "Whew! That sure is a doozy."

I nodded. Jeremiah Donegol motioned me over. He pointed to a carving he was working on. I studied it, and then nodded in appreciation.

"Can't carve with that arm," he said, pointing toward my cast.

I shook my head. "I can't do anything." I took a deep breath and lowered my voice. "Can you cut it off?" I asked. I couldn't bear the thought of missing six more weeks of basketball. Jeremiah's hands were as steady as any doctor's, and if Doctor McNamara wouldn't take off the cast until January, maybe Jeremiah would.

He frowned and shook his head. "Your dad was here already. Warned us you might ask. You got to leave that cast on as long as the doctor says. The arm has to heal."

"We're not going up against your dad," Cal called from across the mill. I wondered how he knew what we were talking about. "Sorry, Andy."

I shrugged and tried not to look too disappointed. "Well, 'bye," I said.

I trudged home and wrote my first basketball article for the *Pierre Journal*. I took it to the newspaper office after school on Tuesday. Mrs. Pickens was messing with a large box on her desk. I cleared my throat and she looked up. "Hello, Andrew. This is my Kodak Brownie. I'm going to photograph the team to print in the newspaper alongside your story. Would you like to see how it works?"

I didn't respond, so she led me to the camera, showing me how to set the shutter and wind the film. I waited until she was finished and then I handed her my story.

"State Tournament Still a Possibility." Mrs. Pickens read the title. She nodded. "Good headline." I waited for her to tell me the Latin root of the word *headline*, but she continued to read.

"Coach Runyon said on Monday that the Carvers still had a chance at the state tournament. 'The other boys on the team are going to have to play above their best,' he said. 'We aren't the same team without the net sniping abilities of Andrew Soaring.'"

I turned away when she read that, but she didn't laugh. She nodded. "That's a good quote," she said. "There are a few grammatical errors, but I'll fix them before I set the type." Mrs. Pickens continued to read.

"The Carvers now have a three-guard lineup, with Lester 'Jug' Lawson to play alongside Hale Brandt and Theodore

Crutcher, Barry 'Stilt' Kline at center, and George Soaring at forward. Rounding out the bench are Neil Waterson and Chadwick 'Wick' Perry.

"With the loss of his brother to injury, George Soaring is the team's top scorer. He did not have any comment about how his brother's injury negatively affects the team, but it's clear that the Carvers need an accurate shooter to play alongside George.

"Andrew expects to return to play in January. Coach thinks the team's chances are 'very good' once he returns. The Carvers are off this weekend, but will return to action on November 30 in the Carvers gym when they play arch-rival Vincennes."

"I tried to get the who, what, when, where, and why in there, like you asked," I said, pointing to the paper. "Sometimes it got a little out of order, though."

"This is well written, Andrew," she said. "I'm quite impressed. Latin *impremere*."

"Just wait until I get this cast off and start playing again."

Mrs. Pickens nodded, tucked my papers into the pocket of her apron, and pulled out a quarter. "Father and Mr. Hammerstein will set this in the linotype, and you will see your first byline in tomorrow's edition of the *Journal*."

I tucked the money into my pocket and hurried out of the newspaper office. I liked the feeling of earning money, but I was only doing this until my arm healed. Playing basketball was my future, not writing about it. And once my arm recovered, nothing could stop me.

Chapter Twenty

Bennie Esposito confronted me before school the following Wednesday morning. His face was streaked with dirt and his clothing was rumpled.

"I didn't do anything to that horse!" he said. He stood in front of me with his fists clenched tightly by his side.

I took a step backward. "I don't know what you're talking about," I lied.

"You broke your arm on your own," Bennie said. "I had nothing to do with it. You should have told AnnaLise that you didn't know how to ride that horse."

"I know how to ride!" I said.

"I didn't cheat!"

We stared at each other for a moment, until I couldn't bear it any longer and looked away. "I thought you were going to be different," Bennie said finally. "But you're not. You're just like every other boy in every other town." He shook his head in disgust. "Scared of everything."

"I'm not scared," I protested. I looked at him again. He curled his upper lip.

"You're all scared," he said.

Bennie smoothed his shirt with his hands, tucked it into his knickers, adjusted his cap, and walked toward the school with his shoulders back and a slight swagger in his step. I followed him. I tried to mimic his swagger but I caught my toe on a clump of dirt and stumbled. I wasn't scared, I thought as I righted myself.

I spent Thanksgiving eating as much as I could to gain my strength back and then going outside to practice a right-handed, one-armed set shot in the cold. I missed every shot. It was the weight of the cast, I told myself. It threw me off balance.

I'd already written a story comparing the Vincennes team to our team. On paper we looked dismal, but I didn't go to practice to see for myself. I didn't want to watch— I wanted to play.

The game was Friday afternoon, so I left for town early and hung out at the drugstore.

Mrs. Pickens found me just as I was getting ready to leave. The other boys in the drugstore snickered when she approached. She was wearing an enormous wool overcoat that looked like a castoff from a giant Merchant Marine.

"Andrew!" she said. "Why didn't you write about the new player in Wednesday's story? Now everybody knows. It's no longer news."

"New player?" I asked, frowning. I looked at the other boys, but they wouldn't meet my eyes.

The door to the drugstore opened, letting in a wave of cold air. It was Ham, followed by his granna and AnnaLise.

"Hi, Andy," Ham called. He walked to the soda fountain. His granna looked around without recognition and waved vaguely in my direction.

"I realize that we aren't as large as some of the big-city papers," Mrs. Pickens was saying, "but we have a reputation to uphold. You must remember, Andrew, the number one rule in journalism is accuracy. You must write with accuracy."

"Yes, ma'am." I started to feel uneasy.

AnnaLise walked toward us. She wore a bright green ribbon in her short hair. "Hello, Mrs. Pickens," she said. She turned to me. "Did you hear about Bennie, Andy? He's going to join the basketball team after all. Now maybe we'll win tonight!"

The tinge of worry in my stomach hardened into a rock.

Mrs. Pickens swept out of the store. I looked at the boys who were still huddled around the soda counter. "Did you know?" I asked. I looked at Ham. "Did you?"

Ham picked up his glass of Coca-Cola from the counter and held it so his granna could take a sip. "I heard that he might."

"Why didn't you tell me?"

Ham shrugged. "I didn't know for sure until just now." He looked at one of the boys. "That means you owe me a quarter, Alvey."

"You bet on whether Bennie would join the basketball team?"

Mrs. Mortimer took another sip of Coca-Cola. Then

she looked around the drugstore. "Is this liquor?" she asked loudly. "I don't want any liquor!"

"Granna!" Ham said. He put his hand on her arm. "It's a Coca-Cola, Granna."

"I don't want any liquor. Felix! No liquor!"

"Granna. It's Ham. Your grandson." He rubbed her shoulder until she calmed down, and then he steered her toward the door.

"I thought you'd be happy Bennie was joining the team," Ham said. "Now we might beat Vincennes." He pointed at a couple of boys before he left. "Fifty cents, Carvers win by at least two. Come on, Granna. Let's go watch the basketball game."

I looked at my arm, at the awful cast, trying not to think what I was thinking. There was only room on a team for two starting forwards. If Bennie played, what would happen to me?

"Who will win?" Mrs. Mortimer sang. She waved her green handkerchief. "Who will win?"

"Carvers Eke Out Win," I wrote on Friday evening after the game. Mrs. Pickens stood in the middle of her office and read the headline of my story. A furrow appeared between her eyebrows. "Despite a lackluster performance against archrival Vincennes, the Pierre boys managed a win Friday night in their own gymnasium, bringing their season total to 2 wins and 2 losses."

Mrs. Pickens skimmed quickly over the play-by-play account of the game, and then read the conclusion. "Although several players managed some key shots, it was obvious that the team was missing something. 'It will be good to have you back,' guard Hale Brandt said to injured player Andrew Soaring.

"Next week the Carvers will pack their grips and head to Smithville, home of the Skibos."

Mrs. Pickens made a clicking noise in her throat. Then she placed the article on her desk and begun pacing back and forth. I watched her with concern.

"You went to the game tonight, did you not?" she asked.

"Yes, ma'am," I said. I had been sitting on a bench just behind the team, next to Earl Blanders, who was in charge of going to the pump and filling the water pitchers.

"So we were watching the same game?"

I nodded again. "Yes, ma'am."

Mrs. Pickens pursed her lips. "What is the first rule in journalism?"

I thought for a moment. "Accuracy?"

"Accuracy! The second rule is clarity. And the third?"

I glanced around the newspaper office, and then shrugged slightly.

"It is accuracy once again!" She flicked my paper. "How many points did Bennie Es . . ."—she checked something on her desk—"Esposito score tonight?"

"Twenty," I said weakly.

"Twenty points!" she exclaimed. She clapped her hands. Then she peered at me. "That's good, isn't it? Some sort of school record?" she asked.

"No, ma'am!" I said quickly. "My brother Pete scored

twenty-six against Gosport his junior year. And I scored twenty against Stinesville in our first game."

"By next Tuesday I want a story," Mrs. Pickens said as if she hadn't heard me. "Tell our readers about Bennie Esposito and what he means to the team."

I tried to nod.

"Does your arm hurt?" Mrs. Pickens asked abruptly.

I had been wiggling the fingers of my left hand and clutching the cast with my right. "No, ma'am," I said. I let my cast, which was in a sling, thump against my stomach.

"Good. Then I will see you next week."

On Tuesday I gave Mrs. Pickens an article about Bennie. She made me rewrite it three times, and then she lectured me about something called objectivity. "You must focus on the object. Remove your personal opinions."

"I don't have any personal opinions," I mumbled.

"Carvers Stand-In New to Basketball," I wrote. "Bennie Esposito, the new player for the Pierre Carvers, got his start shooting baskets in a game-of-chance. His father is currently traveling with their carnival in Florida but will return to Indiana next summer."

Mrs. Pickens didn't say anything more about the story. She led me into the print room and showed me how to slug the type in the linotype machine. When I finally left the newspaper office, I had ink on my good hand and a quarter in my pocket.

By Christmas, when the regular season was half over, our record was eight wins and two losses. Bennie continued to make impossible shots. I hadn't been able to send a basketball through a hoop since November.

On January 4, 1924, Pierre hosted Oolitic and won by a score of forty-eight to twenty-eight. The team was gearing up to play Bloomington.

On January 9, Doc McNamara sawed off my cast.

Chapter Twenty-One

"You'll need to build up the strength in your left arm," the doctor said. "The bones seem solid, and the collarbone knit together beautifully with only a little knot to show it had ever been broken. But the muscles in that arm have weakened from underuse."

I stared at my arm. The skin was pale and puckered. It felt strange, as if it might float off my body like a chicken feather on the wind. I curled my forearm to my shoulder and tried to make a muscle. Nothing.

Dad handed me a shirt. After I broke my arm, Mother had carefully unstitched the left arm from all three of my shirts so they would fit over the cast. Last night she had stitched them all back on. I changed, relishing the strange sensation of fabric against skin. Then I tucked my shirt in my knickers and fastened my suspenders.

I grabbed Pete's basketball and dribbled around the tiny

room filled with the doctor's tools. Then I stopped and took an imaginary shot at the basket.

"Careful, now," the doctor said. He looked at my dad. "Get him chopping wood, carrying water, milking cows. Make him use his left arm. That will build it up." The doctor smiled. "Sure do enjoy reading your articles about the basketball games in the paper," he said. "Makes it seem as if I was right there watching it all over again."

I didn't answer. I was trying to get used to the feel of the ball in my left hand.

My dad nodded. "Thank you, Doc." Then he turned to me. "Get on to school now. Come straight home after basketball practice. You got chores again."

"Yes, sir!" After basketball practice. The words sounded like music. I pulled on my sweater and coat and walked out into the cold. I dribbled my basketball down the street toward the school, until my arm began to ache.

"Andy! You're out of position. Move to your right," Coach yelled.

I looked around in frustration and scooted to the right. George passed me the basketball. I relished the weight of the ball in my hands as I eyed the basket.

"No, Andy! Don't shoot. Pass the ball to Bennie," Coach directed.

Bennie had moved to the top of the court, where he and George changed positions at a run. I passed the ball but misjudged his speed. The ball bounced out of bounds.

"Andy. Come here!" Coach yelled.

I trotted toward him, past my teammates, who took an opportunity to catch their breath, bending forward with their hands on their knees.

"Pass the ball to where he's moving," the coach said. "Not to where he's been." He pointed at the court, waving his hands to illustrate what I should have done.

"Yes, sir," I said. I stretched to try to ease the stitch in my side. My breath came in ragged gasps. "I'm not used to playing back guard, sir. I've always been at forward."

Coach nodded. He summoned the team over. "Let's scrimmage." He sketched positions on a piece of paper. "Andy, you and Bennie at forward take on George and Jug. I'll match up against Stilt." The team chuckled. Coach had at least 100 pounds on Stilt. "Hale, you and Neil go up against Theodore and Wick. Okay, everybody know what you're doing? Practice hard!"

Coach knocked up against him, but Stilt got the tip to Hale, who dribbled down the court and passed it to me. I launched the ball toward the basket. It ricocheted off the rim. George grabbed it, dribbled down the court, and scored. His team gave a whoop before trotting toward the center circle.

"I was open," Bennie said as we gathered at midcourt for the jump. "Jug can't guard me."

We played for thirty minutes. I didn't make a single basket.

After practice I changed in silence, and then walked back into the gym. I lined up at the free-throw line. I missed ten in a row before one finally bounced through the net.

"There you are," George walked toward me. "Come on. We've got to get home."

I shot the ball. It bounced off the rim. George snagged it. I swung my fist and spun around in a circle. "He's playing me at guard!" I said.

George handed me the basketball. "I guess that's what Coach thinks is best."

"I'll never be ready to match up against Bloomington at guard!"

"You can do it, Andy." George paused. "I really want to win this game. The basketball coach from Indiana University might be there."

I didn't want to listen. "I'm going to take the 5:48 home," I said.

I jogged toward the train depot and jumped on the back of the caboose just as it was pulling out of the station. The stationmaster waved as I chugged past. "The arm looks good, Andy," he called. "Let's beat Bloomington."

The train slowed as it approached the edge of our land, closest to the abandoned quarry. The engineer blew two short blasts on the whistle. I hopped off and trudged up the hill toward home.

I helped finish the milking, chopped a cord of wood, and pumped water to fill the animal trough. That night I lay in bed and stared at the frost filigreeing the windowpane. My left arm ached. I pulled it out from under the quilts and let the cold air numb it until I was finally able to fall asleep.

The game against Bloomington at Carver Hall drew a record crowd, with people standing in the doorways next to the bleachers. At halftime, Bloomington was leading sixteen to twelve. "Coach," I said after sitting for twenty minutes. "I'm ready. I can play."

"Not just yet, Andy. I'm leaving Jug in until you're more comfortable at back guard."

"I can play at forward, Coach. I know all the plays. I do."

Coach shook his head and brushed me aside to review strategy with the team.

After the half Bennie went on a shooting streak. I watched the game from the bench, writing the action in my head. "Pierre scores underneath. Bloomington still up 16–14. Esposito and Soaring both score field goals. Esposito drives for two. Bloomington hits two in a row and we're tied. Esposito is fouled, hits both. The score is 22–20. Soaring with the steal. He scores. The noise from the crowd is so deafening that Bloomington calls time. Coach Runyon maintains his lineup with no substitutions."

I gazed into the stands. Dad stood next to two men in suits, who were leaning in to talk to him. Dad was nodding.

Coach looked in that direction. "Coaches," he said as the time-out ended.

"From the university?" I looked at George, who was setting up for the jump ball.

Coach nodded. I considered the two men as play resumed. The university was for rich kids, for town kids and the kids of quarry owners. I knew George was a senior, but he could never leave the farm for college.

With four minutes left to play, Pierre was up by four, but then Bloomington tied it at thirty. Twenty seconds remained, according to Mr. Malcolm, the referee, who kept the time on his pocket watch. Hale passed to Bennie who took a final shot. It sailed cleanly through the hoop. We won thirty-two to thirty! The Pierre crowd cheered, and the Bloomington boys left the court with their heads down.

I wrote the story for the *Pierre Journal*. I felt a stab of fury with every word, with every remembrance of how Coach brushed me off.

On January 12, the day after the win against powerhouse Bloomington, we beat Smithville thirty-seven to thirty-two.

"Coach continues to sideline Soaring," I wrote for Wednesday's edition, highlighting the Smithville win and forecasting the game against Unionville. "Meanwhile, Andrew Soaring maintains he has fully recovered from his injury. Devoted fans are eager to see him return to the lineup."

"Fans?" Mrs. Pickens asked as she removed that sentence from the linotype machine. Mrs. Pickens's father was setting up the flatbed printing press for Wednesday's newspaper run, but even though he had showed me how to work the machine once before, he didn't ask me to stay and help.

I went home, but I didn't really want to be there. Mother looked red-eyed most of the time. I'd overheard Dad telling her that he didn't know how they would afford to buy seed in the spring. She said at least we wouldn't starve. She had canned enough beans and tomatoes to last us through two winters, and we could always butcher another pig. Dad hadn't answered. He spent a lot of time tramping around the abandoned quarry. George got letters in the mail from Indiana University and Wabash College. They were interested. They wanted to talk to him again after the state tournament. The house, except for in the kitchen near the woodstove, was freezing. I could have spent the winter hours after chores and supper shooting baskets, but I didn't. Instead I spent the time cleaning the oil lamps and staring into the fire.

Pierre played four more games and won them all, beating Unionville, Spencer, Williams, and Scircleville.

"Pierre continues their winning streak against smaller schools, but are they ready to compete against big-powers Bedford, Columbus, and Franklin on the road that marches to sectionals?" I wrote.

"George Soaring shows solid play at forward, racking up an impressive number of points in his senior season. Bennie Esposito continues to toss the ball at the basket anytime it hits his hands, often to the detriment of team play. 'Bennie's more of a loner,' teammate Hale Brandt said." I scratched out the rest of his sentence, where he stated that Bennie could be as standoffish as he wanted, as long as he continued to make shots.

"Members of the team have also expressed concerns about Esposito's character. 'He did work for that carnival,' said Kline.

"Why does Coach continue to seat Andrew Soaring on the bench, as it is evident that his shooting abilities have been fully restored?" I concluded the article. "If Coach wants to maintain this winning streak against top contenders, he must stand in favor of solid teamwork and high moral character."

Mrs. Pickens read through the article silently. She narrowed her eyes and tilted her head, as if she was having trouble with her spectacles. Then she placed it on her desk.

"You're a good writer, Andrew."

"Thank you."

She continued without pause. "You have the ability to slant a story any way you like."

"It's all true," I declared. I wondered, for a moment, what Bennie might think when he read the article, but then I shook my head. The story *was* true. I quoted everyone word for word, even if the way I wrote it didn't come across exactly the way they meant it.

"Words are powerful," Mrs. Pickens declared. "Full of intimation."

"Bennie *did* work at a carnival." And I should be Pierre High School's starting forward.

Mrs. Pickens made several slash marks through my story and said she'd need to rework it some before setting it in the linotype.

The next Friday we lost to Bedford forty-eight to forty-six. I interviewed Coach Runyon after the game for the paper and he made it perfectly clear that in spite of the loss, Bennie Esposito would continue to play at forward. "I have to think about what's best for the team, Andrew," he said in clipped, short quotes. I walked away and stared at the words I'd written. *Best for the team?*

Only two more games until sectionals.

I was beginning to hate Bennie Esposito.

Chapter Twenty-Two

On Tuesday afternoon I left the newspaper office and started home. I carried my basketball under one arm and headed down the street, my breath steaming puffs of white in the winter air. I turned at the sound of my name. "Hi, Andy!" AnnaLise called. She and Ham leaned out of their uncle's car and waved.

The Packard thundered to a stop. "Hop in," the sheriff called. "Out of the cold."

I climbed into the rumble seat with Ham. The canvas top of the sheriff's car was up, but since there weren't any windows, the inside wasn't much warmer than it had been outside.

"AnnaLise won't stop talking about the dance party," Ham said. He shook his head.

AnnaLise turned around to face me. "Are you going, Andy?"

152

I wasn't sure how to answer. I vaguely remembered hearing talk about a dance, but I hadn't thought much beyond the game against Columbus on the fifteenth.

"She's gone goo-goo, Andy," Ham said. "Making little valentines and prancing about the house in new party shoes. I liked her better when she only made valentines for her horses."

"The Valentine's Dance," I said, remembering. AnnaLise was making valentines? I flushed, thinking about it, but knowing I'd never have the courage to give her a valentine, not after what happened with the carving.

"I can't wait!" AnnaLise declared. "It's gonna be swell."

"You know I don't approve of these dance parties, AnnaLise," the sheriff said.

"Uncle Felix!"

"It's immoral the way young people carry on. I'm surprised at your parents for agreeing to let you go. I'll have to talk to the Judge," the sheriff said in a disapproving tone. He stopped the car in front of their house. I climbed out with Ham and AnnaLise.

"Get in, Andy," the sheriff said. "I'll drive you home."

"The roads are muddy, sir," I said. "The wagon got stuck two weeks ago, and it took three of us to get it out." As I said that I noticed the frozen mud stuck to the tires of the Packard. Sheriff Mortimer must have gotten stuck, too.

"I was just out that way," the sheriff said. "The roads are fine. Now hop in. It's too cold to walk."

I sat with my basketball in my lap. He put the car in gear. "The Carvers have been playing well," he said.

"Yes, sir."

"I've enjoyed your accounts of the games in the *Pierre Journal.* Mrs. Pickens may be a little off her rocker, but she made a good decision in hiring you."

"Thank you, sir." The cold numbed my face as we barreled down the road. The winter evening was gray, and the gas lamps that lined the street glowed weakly.

"I agree with your analysis of the way the game has been played since you've returned from your injury," he said. He drove quickly, bumping over the gravel roads as we left town. "Sometimes a win isn't all it's cracked up to be." He paused. "I think it's important to win morally as well, don't you agree? For the bewitching of naughtiness doth obscure things that are honest, and the wandering of concupiscence doth undermine the simple mind. From the wisdom of Solomon."

"Yes, sir," I said. I took a deep breath and steeled myself for a sermon. I should have insisted on walking.

"Now, I know Coach Runyon believes his job is to win basketball games, and that is important, but I also think that he has an obligation to ensure that our boys are of noble character."

I didn't answer.

The sheriff turned onto the dirt road that led to our farm. "I don't mind telling you that I have concerns about Bennie Esposito. Not only is he from that carnival," he said it like it was a bad word, "but he is living with his aunt, Teresa Ricci, who takes in boarders that are known drunkards. 'They reel to and fro, and stagger like a drunken man, and are at their wits' end.'"

"Sir?"

"From the Psalms. I don't want to burden you with matters of law enforcement, Andy, but I know that writing for the newspaper and playing for the basketball team give you a certain access to information that I simply don't have. I also want you to know that there may be a monetary reward for any information about the carnies and the Italians of Vigo Quarry."

"Monetary reward?" I exclaimed.

The sheriff looked at me. "Enough to help your family." He paused for a moment before continuing. "If you find anything, anything at all, you come to me first," he said. "Then you may go to the paper. Do we have a deal?"

I nodded, uncertain as to what I was promising. "Yes, sir."

"Good." The sheriff opened the door to his car. "Now, go eat your supper. You have to build your strength. Sectionals are coming."

On Thursday, Valentine's Day, I slicked down my hair with water and dressed in long pants. Mother heated several flatirons on the stove and used them to iron my shirt until it was crisp. I left for school early, jogging down the frozen, rutted roads toward Ham's house. I arrived just as he and AnnaLise and their two younger sisters were leaving.

"Hi, AnnaLise," I said. I took off my cap and tried to smooth my hair, but then pulled my hand away sharply. Icicles! My hair had frozen. I quickly replaced my cap.

"Hey, Andy," Ham said. "What are you doing here?"

The two little girls glanced at me.

"Uh, AnnaLise," I said as we walked toward the school-house, "I've been meaning to tell you." I stumbled over the words. My tongue felt thick. "You know a while back, in November, before I tried to ride Jalahar. . . ?"

"I really am sorry about that, Andy. But it was so long ago," AnnaLise said. "I did hope you'd have forgiven me by now."

"Yes, sure, I did, but that's not what—"

"I made something for you." She smiled. "Wait just a minute." She opened a book and rifled through it. She pulled out a pink paper heart. "This is for you."

The little girls laughed. Ham sputtered.

I ignored them and studied the heart. In tiny letters she had printed, "For You, Valentine." I grinned and forgot what I had been trying to tell her. "Thank you," I said. "It's real pretty." We arrived at the school. She waved and walked through the east doors. I stared after her until Ham shoved me toward the other entrance.

Later that day, during mathematics, I saw Bennie staring at a valentine that he had tucked between the pages of his book. I leaned forward to get a closer look. It was large and red, with lace trim. The words printed in the middle of the heart read, "Dear Bennie, Be My Valentine. Always, AnnaLise."

I sat back in my seat feeling as if I had just gotten the air knocked out of me. I excused myself from class, went outside, and tossed my pink valentine into the privy.

After Friday's basketball game, a close win against Columbus, I met my parents outside the gymnasium. "I might be home late," I said, thinking murderously of Bennie, who had just scored eighteen points to my two. "I have to . . . I have work to do. At the newspaper office." That was partly true. I just didn't mention what I was going to do after I turned in my story.

Dad nodded without question. "I appreciate everything you've been doing," he said. "The money you've been earning . . . it's been a help." He put a hand on my shoulder.

A knot formed in my throat. I suddenly wished that I was still little. I wanted to lean against his chest, snuggle into the wool of his overcoat, and be told that everything was going to be all right. But just then George joined us, and the moment was lost.

I turned in my story to Mrs. Pickens and then tracked down Ham at the drugstore. He was eating a dish of ice cream covered with chocolate and nuts. "You've got to try this, Andy," he said through a mouthful. "It's called an ice cream sundae. It's the bee's knees!"

"Not right now," I said. I waited until he finished his last bite, and then I pulled him outside. "Come on. I've got something I have to do, and I need your help."

"What is it?" he asked as he trotted after me down Main Street and across Homestead toward the edge of town and the Vigo Quarry.

"I don't know exactly, but I'll bet you the cost of your ice cream sundae that whatever it is, it's going to help me get back my starting spot on the basketball team."

Chapter Twenty-Three

"So where are we going, anyway?" Ham asked as we left behind the lights of the town and skirted the dark, rutted country roads.

I told Ham about my conversation with his uncle on Tuesday. "Somebody's getting those men drunk, and the sheriff thinks it might be Bennie's aunt."

Ham whistled. "Willard Nevil told me that alcohol's near as easy to buy now as it was before Prohibition, but he won't ever tell me how to get it. You really think Bennie and his aunt are making moonshine?"

"Making it or bootlegging it," I said. Now that the idea had taken hold, I was starting to believe it. I just had to find the evidence to convince everyone else.

"Judge hates bootleggers. Says alcohol's the root of all evil. It's what caused Grandpa to get so mean before he died." Ham paused for a minute. "I shouldn't have said that," he said. "The Judge . . . he wouldn't want anyone to know."

I frowned. Everyone knew Old Man Mortimer had been a mean drunk back in his day, but no one ever talked about it. "'S'okay," I said.

"Trouble with bootleggers," Ham said, changing the subject without a missed beat, "is they're so hard to catch."

"They've got to hide it somewhere," I said. What if Bennie's aunt was running hooch, and we found it? She'd go to jail. And everyone in town would consider Bennie guilty by association. After all, he lived with her. No one would care how many points he could score or how great a player he was. He'd be suspended from school and kicked off the team.

The road to the Vigo Quarry was about half a mile outside of town. Since it bordered the back of our land, I knew it well. I took loping strides, leaving the gravel road and cutting across a dark, frozen pasture. I had forgotten to bring a lantern, but a half-moon shone overhead. Ham took two steps for every one of mine. It wasn't long before he was panting and complaining that his side hurt.

Our boots thudded on the frozen ground. A chill wind tugged at our coats. We walked along the edge of the quarry road, taking care to skirt the quarry itself, until we saw a cluster of houses.

We approached the Ricci boarding house from behind. An old Model T was parked in the yard. Ham nudged me, pointing out the car. I nodded. That's where we'd start looking. Whenever a car sped too fast down Main Street Ham liked to bet it was someone running moonshine. The fact that it was parked in the yard, instead of in a barn for the winter, was suspicious. We crept closer, moving from tree to tree. When we were about twenty yards from the car, we stopped behind a low hedge. From our position we could see the front door. The house was quiet. I saw a lamp shining from one of the windows, and in the air I could smell wood smoke from the chimney.

"Now what do we do?" Ham asked.

I frowned. I hadn't thought that far ahead. "Shh!" I hissed. I gauged the distance between us and the car, and then between the car and the house.

Ham was quiet for a moment. Then I heard him stomping his feet. He huffed into his hands and rubbed them together. "It's cold," he said. Then, "Do you have anything to eat? I'm hungry."

"Shh!" I hissed again, but my stomach was rumbling, too, and I was starting to wonder what I was doing there. Would we have to wait all night, watching to see if Mrs. Ricci would load up her car with alcohol? Could we arrest her if she did? Or should we just search the car ourselves?

The tip of my nose started to freeze. We couldn't stay here too much longer. "Wait here," I whispered. I crouched low to the ground and eased toward the car. Ham followed.

I ducked around the car to the side farthest from the house. I stood and peered into the back of the car. "It doesn't have a back seat!" I whispered. But I couldn't see much else. It was too dark. I put my hand on the door handle and lifted. The door opened with a loud groan.

Behind me I could sense Ham stiffen. "Hurry up!" he whispered.

I crawled into the car and started to feel around. The back of the car smelled like pine and dirt. I touched what felt like a large, wooden box. "I found something!" I whispered. I reached up and pried off the top of the box. It creaked.

"Who's there?" I froze, and then tried to creep out of the car. A figure stood on the front porch. "Who's out there?" I heard the unmistakable click of a bullet being loaded into a rifle chamber.

"Andy!" Ham was crouched behind the car, bouncing from side to side.

I scurried from the car and fell to the ground next to him.

The rifle boomed and a bullet whined into the air.

Ham scrambled backward. A twig snapped under his foot. The rifle swung in our direction as another figure joined the woman on the porch. It was Bennie. "What is it?" he asked. His aunt didn't answer. Instead I heard the rifle open and another bullet being loaded into a chamber. "Run!" I screamed.

Chapter Twenty-Four

We bolted toward the woods, running as fast as we could in no particular direction. We ran until we were surrounded by trees and could no longer see the oil lamps of the Italian neighborhood. I slowed to a stop. I knew the area was dotted with quarries and sinkholes, and we were just as likely to fall to our deaths as be shot. Ham was gasping great lungfuls of air, and my side had cramped in a knot of pain. Ham reached over and clutched his knees.

"Where are we?" Ham asked once he caught his breath.

I looked around. Trees stretched in every direction, their leafless branches doing their best to obscure the light from the moon. "I don't know," I said. I hadn't paid attention to which direction we'd been running.

"Do you think we're near the quarry?" he asked. I could see the whites of his eyes glinting in the moonlight.

"I hope not." We had heard the stories, since we were

little, about people who had unknowingly plunged over the side of a quarry and fallen fifty feet to their death.

"What are we gonna do?" Ham asked.

"Start walking, I guess. We'll find our way out eventually."

Ham made a noise in the back of his throat. Well, maybe he wouldn't find his way out, I thought, but if I kept walking I'd eventually figure out where I was.

"What was in the box?" Ham asked after we had trudged for a few minutes. "Was it moonshine?"

"I don't think so." I sighed. I knew they were brewing moonshine, I just knew it. But I hadn't found anything to prove it.

"So what was it?"

"Potatoes." In the brief moment after I'd gotten the lid off the box and reached inside, I'd felt the unmistakable texture of spuds.

"Potatoes?" Ham laughed.

I frowned. "It's got to be there somewhere."

"Hey, look!" Ham stopped walking and pointed. An old building stood ten feet in front of us, nestled in the trees. "It's a barn or something. Maybe now we can figure out where we are." Ham walked toward the building.

"It's too small to be a barn," I said, following him. "And who puts a barn in the woods?" But the building looked familiar, and the thought niggled in the back of my mind that I knew this place.

Ham opened the door with a flourish. "Smells funny," he said before venturing inside.

It did smell funny, I thought, as I followed him. It was sour and rich, like when Mother left the yeast starter for the bread out too long.

"Open that door a little wider," Ham said. "I can't see a thing." He started feeling his way around the room, but then he stopped and whistled. "Come here, Andy. Would you look at this? I think we hit pay dirt."

Ham yanked me toward him and then grabbed my hand and put it on what felt like a large barrel. The bottom of the barrel felt warm. At the top, something round and smooth curled up and around, dripping into what felt like a mason jar. The smell of sour yeast grew stronger.

I pulled back and stared into the darkness. "What is it?"

Ham continued to pat around on the floor. I heard him pick up something and then I heard the sound of metal against metal. Ham was quiet for a moment, and then, "Whoeee!" he said, coughing. He thrust something cold and smooth into my hands. "Try this."

It was some sort of bottle. I held it under my nose and drew back at the smell. "Try it," Ham said.

I put the bottle to my lips, which began to burn. "What is it?"

"It's whiskey," Ham said. "Come on, just try one sip. It's not so bad. You'll see."

I tilted the bottle and let a drop fall on my tongue. I shuddered but then swallowed. The taste burned my throat until I started coughing. Ham pounded me on the back. "See," he said. "Isn't it awful?"

"It's terrible!" My stomach felt warm, and soon the warmth spread to my arms and legs. Ham handed me the top and I screwed it back on the bottle.

"Do you know what this means? It means that thing in the corner must be a still! Someone must come out here to get the hooch."

We must have had the same thought at the same time because we both scrambled out of the building.

As we left, I suddenly realized why the building seemed so familiar. I glanced around the side of the shack, hoping not to see what I knew was there. Ten feet up, at the top of the wall, there was a basketball hoop.

I grabbed Ham before he could look and hustled him away from the building. "Come on," I said. "We'd better get out of here."

"I'm so lost," Ham whispered as I pulled him through the woods. "How are we ever going to get home, let alone tell Uncle Felix how to find this place?"

I shook my head. "I don't care about telling anyone. I just want to get home." Little did Ham know I knew exactly where we were.

Chapter Twenty-Five

I led Ham in large, looping circles, eventually tracking back the way we came, past the Vigo Quarry. As soon as Ham saw the cluster of houses he gasped. "I know where we are," he whispered as we crept past Teresa Ricci's boarding house, keeping a close eye on the front porch. "The still isn't far from these houses. I'll bet you a dollar that hooch belongs to Bennie's aunt."

It was a bet he'd lose. I realized I was still holding on to the bottle. I quickly stuck it in my pocket. When we reached the road I pointed. "That's the way toward town," I told Ham. "Can you find your way back to your house from here?"

"Where are you going?"

"Home," I said. "I'm tired." I was.

"When should we tell Uncle Felix?"

"I don't know how to find that still again," I lied. "Do you?"

Ham shook his head. "Not really. But it's got to belong to someone who lives by the Vigo Quarry, doesn't it?" Ham whistled. "Let's go looking for it again," he said. "This time in the daylight."

"Maybe after sectionals," I said, knowing that I wouldn't take Ham back to that shack ever again if I could help it. "Just . . . don't tell the sheriff or the Judge anything until we figure out where it is and decide what to do."

Ham agreed. He walked toward the direction of town and I trudged to the farm. When I got home the grandfather clock in the corner chimed midnight. No one else stirred. I tiptoed to my room and crawled into bed. But I didn't sleep. I spent most of the night thinking. My mind kept spinning around the still in the shack—my shack. I thought of Dad's worries about the mortgage, and the sheriff's long ago statement, which I hadn't understood until that moment, about folks using corn to ferment their own cash crop. Worrisome explanations niggled the back of my mind.

The next morning I did my chores in a daze. The temperature had climbed into the fifties by afternoon, and Mother wanted to beat the rugs. I helped her carry them to the clothesline, where we beat them with a broomstick. It was itchy and dirty, but the hard work took my mind off my thoughts.

After supper Mother cleared the table and washed the dishes in the wash pan. I filled a pot with water from the pump and heated it on the stove. Then I poured the hot water into the tub in the washroom and, shivering in the cold air, crawled into the tub with a bar of Lifebuoy soap for my Saturday evening bath.

167

"Aren't you going to the dance party?" I asked George after we finished bathing. I didn't feel well, I didn't want to go, but I couldn't bear to stay home and wonder if AnnaLise was dancing with Bennie.

George shook his head. He didn't look up. "No."

I put on my shirt. The room was cold and the fingers in my left hand felt stiff. I had trouble getting them around the buttons. "Why not?"

George frowned. "It's not appropriate," he said.

I snorted. "Not appropriate? Who talks like that?" I made a face. Then, "Besides, I heard that Betty Stidwell is sweet on you." I knew George liked her. I'd seen the way he looked at her during lunch when she passed by.

George caught his breath. "Dance parties are . . ." he paused, as if he was battling with himself. "Immoral."

"Immoral? You sound like Sheriff Mortimer. It's a dance. It won't kill you to have a little fun." I pulled the ends of the bow tie around my neck and thought that with how I was feeling, the last thing I wanted to do was have fun.

"Well, the sheriff would know," George said sharply. "He told me about the dangers of dance parties just last night—the dangers of immorality. He told me that's why Pete left for the war." Then George pinched his lips as if he'd said too much.

I stared at my brother. "What?"

George looked away. "Never mind," he said. "It doesn't matter."

"What?" I yelled. "What did the sheriff say? Why did Pete leave?"

George looked torn. "The sheriff said Pete was a victim of immorality, and that he felt like he had to leave, until people forgot."

"Forgot what?" A cold, hard weight lodged in my chest. "Until they forgot what, George?"

"I think . . . I mean . . . it could happen to anybody." George's eyes were wide and worried. "We have to be careful, Andy. It's for our own good." George set his face into a stiff mask.

I slowly finished tying my bow tie and then I smoothed my hair with the palm of my hand. It couldn't be true. Not Pete. Not my Pete. If only he were here, he would explain everything. He would fix everything.

I gave my bow tie one last tug and then walked out of the room without saying another word.

Chapter Twenty-Six

I felt dazed as I walked with Ham toward the school gymnasium, where the dance party was being held.

Ham nudged me. "So, who?" he asked.

I looked at him blankly. "Huh?"

"I asked you three times—who do you want to dance with?" We walked into the gymnasium. The wood floor was covered with a tarpaulin and the room had been decorated with paper hearts. Hundreds of them.

"No one," I muttered.

"Oh, come on." Ham snickered. "Who's your girl?" Ham poked me in the shoulder.

I stepped away. "No one," I yelled.

People around us said, "Shhh!" At the front of the room, the members of the Pierre Symphonic Band were warming up.

I shouldn't have come. George was right.

The band started to play. "Let's hang up our coats," Ham said.

I followed him to the coatrack, which was behind the refreshment table. Then we found a spot along the wall with some of the other boys. The girls, wearing brightly colored dresses, crowded in a bunch against the other wall.

"Nice party. Isn't this a nice party?" Stilt Kline asked. He pulled at his starched white collar uncomfortably and then studied his shoes.

The band finished one song. I clapped half-heartedly and they started another. Several of the adult chaperones walked to the middle of the floor and began to waltz. Across the gymnasium, I saw AnnaLise talking to a couple of her girlfriends.

We watched in silence as the grown-ups danced more songs. Then a couple of girls broke away from the group and went to talk to the band director. The band leader nodded. AnnaLise and one of her friends rushed across the gymnasium toward Ham. "They're going to play the Charleston. Come on! Dance with us! Please. No one is dancing."

Ham grinned. "I'll dance," he said, taking the friend's hand. "It'll be swell. Come on, Andy."

"I don't want to," I said sharply.

AnnaLise's face fell. I wanted to melt into the floor.

"I would be honored to dance with you, AnnaLise," said a voice behind me. I turned to see Bennie Esposito. Anna-Lise grinned. She grabbed Bennie's hand and pulled him to the middle of the dance floor.

"Whoa, Andy. You let that one go," Stilt Kline said.

"Be quiet, Stilt." I moved off into the corner, and stood with my hands folded across my chest, watching the dancers.

When the song ended, Ham broke away from the dancers and headed toward the refreshment table. I met him there.

"I can't believe you let him dance with your sister," I said through clenched teeth. I looked across the gymnasium, to where AnnaLise was still talking to Bennie. Another song began, and they continued to dance. "Why didn't you tell her to stay away from him? After, you know, last night."

Ham took a cup of punch. "I tried." He drained the glass. "She threatened to beat me up."

I glared at him. He had a red mustache above his upper lip. "She's your sister!"

Ham looked apologetic. "We don't know for sure that the still really *does* belong to Bennie's aunt—"

"Ham!"

"Aww, Andy . . ."

I grabbed my coat from the rack behind the refreshment table. "I'm going home."

"You're going home? Already? You just got here." Ham poured himself another cup of punch. "This is good, Andy. You should have some."

I scowled. My head ached. I tried to wrestle into my coat, but the sleeve was stuck. Ham finished his punch and set the cup on the table. I gave my coat another tug. Something fell out of my pocket and landed on the floor with a heavy clank. I looked at the shiny, silver bottle in alarm, and then looked at Ham. He wasn't paying attention. I stared at the object on the ground as if it was a rattler, poised to strike.

I had forgotten it was still in my pocket. Had anybody else seen what had happened? I held my breath and inched closer. I'd have to grab it.

"Just stay for the next one," Ham hollered over the band. As he yelled the last word the band stopped playing. His voice echoed through the gym in the half-second between the band's last note and the applause from the dancers. Then the punch bowl, and the flask, was surrounded.

I took several rapid steps backward, away from the silver bottle still lying on the floor. I bumped into someone and turned rapidly, apologizing.

"Sorry, oh sorry, Coach Runyon," I said quickly.

"Leaving already?" Coach asked.

I pulled on the front of my coat. "Yes. That is, yes. I was leaving. Am leaving. I need my rest, right?" I tried to keep one eye on Coach and one eye on what was happening at the punch bowl. So far no one had noticed the bottle.

"Have you seen all the trophies?" I asked. "They're over there—look—right over there in the case. Maybe we could get our own trophy, wouldn't that be great?"

I kept looking back toward the refreshment table as I tried to steer Coach Runyon toward the trophies. Then I paused, staring intently at the group of teachers along the wall closest to the refreshment table. Mr. Harcour, the principal, suddenly stopped talking to Mr. Willeby, the science teacher. I saw Mr. Harcour's eyes widen.

No. I thought. *No, no, no.*

Mr. Harcour took several long strides toward the refreshment table. He reached down, picked up the flask, straightened, and unscrewed the lid. He waved the flask under his nose and then drew back. His face tightened as he screwed the lid back onto the flask. He marched quickly out of the room.

"Hey, Andy," Ham called, walking toward me. "I think I drank too much punch. I'm going to the privy."

I grabbed Ham's arm and nearly pulled him over in my haste to get outside. "Me too! Good-bye, Coach!"

Chapter Twenty-Seven

Sunday passed in a haze. On Monday morning I woke early. I knew that Mr. Harcour would be waiting at the school with questions about the flask.

Whose was it, really? Did anyone know I had been the one who dropped it? Could it belong to my dad? The still was on our property, but I just couldn't believe it was Dad's. But if it wasn't his, then whose? The answers floated in the back of my mind, just out of reach.

The barn smelled of hay and manure and a grassy, bovine scent. The sky outside was still dark, with only a faint gray lining the eastern horizon. Inside the barn, coal oil lanterns flickered. One cow stamped and another lowed. It was a contrast to the early morning crash of stone against stone and the roar of saw blades that started the day in a quarry.

"Why did Pete leave?" I asked suddenly, when we were halfway through the milking. Dad was milking the cow next to mine. George was on the other side of the barn. Somehow all the questions about Pete and the questions I had about the still and even the ones about Bennie had become tangled in my mind. If I could sort out one strand, I thought, maybe I could figure out the others.

Dad sat back on his stool. His jaw clenched. I thought maybe he wouldn't answer, that he would refuse to talk about Pete. A stream of milk shot into his pail, splashing against the sides before swirling around the bottom. "He was a brave boy," he said finally, as if reading lines from a book. "He wanted to fight for his country."

"What's the other reason? Why else did he leave?"

"Who have you been talking to, Andrew? Has Mrs. Pickens. . . ?"

"No." I wondered, all at once, what the newspaper editor knew and why I'd never asked her. "She didn't tell me anything." I finished milking my cow, but I didn't move. "Is it true? Did Pete leave because of Claudia?"

"Claudia?"

"Pete didn't have to leave. We could have helped him take care of the baby!"

"What baby?" Dad asked. He pulled away from the cow and looked at me with wide eyes. "There was no baby!"

"But . . ." I felt George come up behind me, listening, but he didn't say a word.

"Claudia wasn't . . ." Dad looked pained. "You thought Claudia was . . . ? Why would you think something like that?"

"The sheriff said Pete was a victim," George said. "Of immorality."

Dad's voice choked. I watched in horror as a tear rolled

176

down his face. I had never before seen him cry. Never. Not even when Pete died. "Felix!" A vein in Dad's forehead throbbed. "Pete didn't do anything wrong. Nothing! He was a good boy. A brave boy. He left for the war because he wanted to fight for something he believed in! He wanted to do what was right."

"But . . ." I blinked. Bits of information started to piece together in my head. The newspaper announcement about Mother and Dad's wedding. Mrs. Mortimer saying that Pete was an early baby.

"You and Mother didn't get married until February? Did you?" I asked. And Pete had been born in August.

Dad bowed his head. "We married," he said simply. "Pete wasn't illegitimate." Dad's shoulders shook. I tentatively put my hand on his back until the shaking subsided. "He was a good boy." Dad stood, filling the barn with his bulk. "I want you boys to know one thing. You may make mistakes in your life, you may even do some things that are really wrong. That happens. But then I expect you to do whatever you have to do to fix those mistakes. You hear me? Now get to school."

George and I finished our chores. We walked to town in silence. I left him and went into the newspaper office.

"Mrs. Pickens!" I said. She was sitting at her desk, wearing a large, red tam-o'-shanter on her head. The pom-pom on top bobbed when she looked up. "May I borrow your camera?" I asked urgently. In my head, the pieces of the puzzle were crashing violently into position. I wasn't sure what I needed to do, but I needed to do something.

"Should I inquire as to the reason?" she asked.

"No, ma'am," I said. "Not yet. I don't . . . I don't know what's going to happen."

She nodded. "You may. I understand that something is happening at the high school?"

"Yes, ma'am. I . . ." I paused. "I don't know what's going to happen with that, either."

"Might there be a newsworthy story?"

"Yes, ma'am." I thought about the flask and the still and the rest of the basketball season and everything that could happen in the next few hours. "Yes, ma'am, there might."

"The number one rule in journalism?" she asked.

I answered without hesitation. "Accuracy." I picked up the Kodak Brownie and started toward the door, but then I turned. "Mrs. Pickens? Did you know about Pete? About Mother and Dad and why they got married in February but told everyone they married in December?"

"Yes," Mrs. Pickens said, looking down at her papers. "I knew."

"But you never said . . ."

"No." She shook her head. The pom-pom on her hat wobbled. "It wasn't newsworthy, Andrew. After many years in the newspaper business, I have learned that some stones are better left unthrown."

I arrived at the school in time to see Sheriff Mortimer walk through the front door. Students were gathered in groups around the school yard. Ham broke away from a group and walked quickly toward me. At the edge of the yard I saw Bennie, standing alone.

"The principal found a flask at the dance Saturday night!" Ham said. "Mr. Harcour told everyone to stay out here. He's been calling people in one by one."

I looked around at the groups of students. A low, excited buzz filled the school yard. I saw AnnaLise standing with her girlfriends. Her face was red and blotchy.

"Uncle Felix asked me this morning if I knew anything about it." Ham's eyes were wide. "I didn't want to let on that you . . . that we . . ." Ham looked around. "You left the bottle we found at the shack, didn't you? I mean, that wasn't the same one?"

I didn't answer.

"Uncle Felix thinks the flask belongs to Bennie."

"He does?"

Ham nodded. "Everybody does."

The door to the school opened. Everyone stopped talking and looked. Mr. Harcour stood in the doorway.

"Bennie Esposito," he called. "Come here, please."

I watched Bennie walk into the school. I left the camera with Ham and followed.

"Andrew?" Mr. Harcour said as I walked into the principal's office. Judge Mortimer, Coach Runyon, Mr. Harcour, Mr. Malcolm, and Sheriff Mortimer were seated in a row facing Bennie. "This is a private meeting. We will issue a statement to the newspaper once we have made a determination."

"I'm not here for the newspaper," I said. "I'm here for me."

"Andrew!" Coach Runyon looked pained. "The basketball

team, the school body, everybody will find out what is happening once we have finished our investigation."

"Yes, sir." I blanched under the weight of their eyes. I knew, knew without any doubt, that these five men would find Bennie guilty. Bennie would be expelled from school, he would go back to his carnival, and Coach would put me in as starting forward. Sectionals started in two weeks. Enough time for me to get my shot back. Plenty of time. It was something I wanted more than almost anything.

I looked at Bennie as I turned to go. His face was impassive. His dark eyes looked straight ahead, unflinching. I put my hand on the doorknob. The silence grew.

"Sir?" I said, looking back toward Mr. Harcour.

"What is it, Andrew?"

I let go of the doorknob. "The flask isn't his, sir."

"What?"

I turned toward the men. As I spoke, I studied each of their faces. "The flask that you found at the dance, it isn't Bennie's. It's mine."

Chapter Twenty-Eight

The school board questioned me, but I didn't offer much information. As I studied the men, the rest of the puzzle fit firmly into place. I knew the flask wasn't mine, and I was fairly certain that one of those men knew it, too.

"Go home now, Andrew," Mr. Harcour said finally. "I would ask that you not return to school until we've had an opportunity to consider disciplinary action."

I left the school without a word. Ham questioned me when I took the camera from him. "The still we found doesn't belong to Bennie's aunt," I said.

Ham trotted after me. "It doesn't? Whose is it then?"

I couldn't answer. Not without proof. I left him staring after me, and headed home, skirting the house and following the barren fields toward the western edge of our property.

I lugged the camera through the woods, carrying the heavy Brownie with both hands. I hoped I was right. I didn't want to think about what would happen if I was wrong.

The day was gray, the color of steel, and hung thick with the last grasp of winter. I set up the camera and tried to remember what Mrs. Pickens had shown me. I wished I'd paid more attention. Set the shutter, wind the film. Fix the aperture, focus the lens. It seemed so complicated.

In the distance, I heard the sound of an automobile. I took stock of my position, well hidden by the trees. I could still see everything that I needed to see and capture it with the camera. Camouflaged. I knew what the word meant, but not its origins.

I wished the still belonged to Bennie. I wished the flask had belonged to him, too. Everyone already wanted to believe it was his.

I knew that if I wanted to I could write this story to make Bennie look guilty. I also knew that no matter how well I wrote, it wouldn't make it true.

The automobile grew louder. I could hear it jolting over the ruts in the frozen road. I crouched behind the camera, which was as wide as my head, and peered through the lens.

The automobile stopped. I heard a car door open, and then slam shut.

Who, what, when, where, why, and how. I ran through the list of questions in my head. I thought I knew the answers to them all. But I needed proof.

A door creaked open. Through the lens I saw a figure enter the shack. There was a spark, and then the inside of the shack was illuminated with a soft glow. The figure walked out of the shack, carrying a box. From the sounds, I guessed he loaded the box in the back of his automobile. Come on, I thought, show me something.

More boxes were loaded into the car. Behind the camera I bit my lip until I tasted blood.

The figure entered the shack again. I heard a loud gurgling sound, a thump, and then the sound of clinking glass. The smell of sour yeast hung heavy in the chill air.

Even if I captured this with the camera, would anyone believe me?

The man, with his back to me, tugged on something. I could hear it scrape across the floor. When he reached the doorway he tripped and swore. He stood upright and turned. I could see the expression on his face. He had plans for that still, I thought. It might wind up at Bennie's house yet. I could leave now and pretend that I had nothing to do with it.

The man leaned against the doorjamb. I could see the still behind him, illuminated in the glow of the lantern. He pulled a silver flask from his pocket, uncorked the lid, and took a sip.

I squeezed the shutter. The camera clicked and the flashpan popped.

The man froze and then turned toward the noise. He took a step in my direction. "Who's there?"

I scrambled backward into the woods, trying to protect the camera.

"I know someone's there. Come out!"

I hid the camera carefully, took a deep breath, and then walked toward the shack. "Sheriff Mortimer," I said. "It *is* you."

"Andrew!" the sheriff said. "What are you doing here? Why aren't you at home? Mr. Harcour and the Judge are on their way to talk to your parents. You are in a lot of trouble, young man."

"Ham and I, we found the flask. Here. In this shack." I walked toward him as I spoke.

"Why didn't you tell me?" The sheriff looked concerned. "I have been looking for this moonshining operation for a long time. You could have been in a lot of danger if the bootleggers came back while you were here."

"I wanted them to come back," I said. "I wanted to catch them. I'm going to write about it for the paper."

The sheriff's eyes hardened as he studied me. "Well, you're lucky I got here first," he said. "Bootleggers can be extremely dangerous. You might have been hurt." He laughed. It was a strange, tight sound.

"The boxes, they're full of bottles, aren't they? Your bottles."

"What are you saying, Andrew? Those boxes are evidence. I'm going to confiscate this still and then I'm going to press charges." The sheriff looked around. "Why, we're on your father's land, aren't we?"

"Yes, sir," I said. "Land that you are renting." I continued to talk, piling up the accusations. "Your mother, Mrs. Mortimer, she was the one who told me that you have a problem with drinking. I thought she was just talking crazy, but—"

"Andrew!" The sheriff moved toward me.

"It still didn't make sense until today, at the school. I saw the look on your face. My dad would never . . . but you would."

"Why, you little . . ." the sheriff moved toward me: I

sidestepped him. "You're a fool," he said, moving back into the shack. "You should have let Bennie take the blame. Now you're the one who will be expelled. You'll bring shame on your family."

He picked up his lantern and brushed off his suit. "No one will ever believe you, Andrew. I'm the sheriff. The sheriff! What are you? Nothing but a second-string basketball player and a dirt-poor farmer's kid." He turned away from me.

"I took a picture."

The words hung in the air for a moment, and then the sheriff wheeled around as if he was going to come after me. But his toe caught the edge of a warped board. He stumbled. The lantern fell out of his hand and crashed against the still.

Coal oil spilled onto the floor, and the flame from the lantern raced after it.

"Fire!" I yelled. The sheriff pulled himself to his feet and stared at the flames.

"Andrew!" The sheriff was tugging on the still, trying to move it. "Help me get this out of here."

"Sheriff Mortimer!" I screamed. "It's going to catch fire." I could see the flames behind him, devouring the burlap bags, burning the dry wood of the shack. There was alcohol in that still. In a minute the whole thing would go up. "You've got to get out of there!"

He pushed at the still, wild-eyed, but then stumbled to the doorway. The fire crackled and popped, licking the edge of the barrel. I started running as the barn erupted. Sparks rocketed upward and littered the air around us. I buried my face in my arm. Behind me, I heard the sheriff scream. I turned. The tail of his overcoat was on fire. He raced around in circles, yelling. I ran toward him and knocked him down, trying to smother the flames against the ground. The sheriff grabbed my arm and twisted, rolling me over and pinning me on my stomach. He pulled my arm behind me.

"Ow," I screamed. "Let go!"

"I'll break it again," he said. "If you breathe a word of this to anybody, I'll break it so it'll never heal!"

I arched my back and rolled, but he held tight. Pain shot up my arm.

In the noise and panic of the moment, I didn't hear the car until it was nearly upon us. There were voices, yelling, and then someone pulled the sheriff off me.

The Judge had the sheriff in a hammerlock. Ham rushed toward me, followed by my dad.

"Andy!" Ham looked at his uncle, who was being wrestled into the car. "What's going on?"

"How did you get here?" I asked. I massaged my sore arm.

Dad pulled me away from the heat of the flames. "When you left school, after you told the school board that the flask belonged to you, Ham told the Judge that he was with you when you found it. He led us here."

Behind us, I could hear the popping of the fire.

"Sorry it took so long," Ham grimaced. "I couldn't exactly remember where it was. But we saw the flames from the Italian neighborhood. Teresa Ricci telephoned the fire brigade."

"It wasn't really my flask," I said. "I mean, I did bring it to the dance, but it wasn't mine. It belongs . . ." I looked at my dad, hoping he'd believe me. "It belongs to the sheriff."

I heard a roar, and looked to see the new fire truck barreling down the Vigo Quarry Road toward us.

Ham looked at me, then at the burning shack, then at his father's car. "What? You mean the still . . . ? It belongs to . . . ?"

"Sheriff Mortimer," I said.

"Uncle Felix," Ham said. He shook his head. "Whoa. Andy. I guess I should have . . . I mean . . . I'm sorry."

We stood in silence for a few minutes and watched the fire brigade douse the shack with water. The flames hissed under the combined assault of water and cold.

"I better go," Ham said after the Judge had settled Sheriff Mortimer in the back of his car. "Bye, Andy."

Dad put his arm around my shoulders as we watched them drive away. "It was foolish, not coming to us when you found that still."

"Yes, sir."

"But you did a good thing, too, telling the school board what you did. I'm . . ." his voice cracked. I looked at him in alarm, but he wasn't crying. He was smiling. "I'm proud of you, Son."

Chapter Twenty-Nine

I left for school early the next morning, before dawn. I needed to stop by the newspaper office to give the camera and my story to Mrs. Pickens, but there was something else I wanted to do first.

The school was unlocked. I pushed open the doors to the gymnasium and heard the familiar thump of basketball against hardwood. My footsteps echoed in the dim, nearly deserted space.

"George said you got to school early."

Bennie caught the basketball and spoke without looking at me. "Franklin on Friday. Then sectionals. I need to practice." He eyed the hoop, bent his knees, and shot. The basketball swished through. I grabbed it off the bounce and tossed it back.

"Thank you," Bennie said as he caught the ball. "For telling them about the flask."

"It wasn't yours." I took a breath. "I'm . . . well . . . I wanted to . . ." I reached into my pocket and fumbled for a moment, rustling past Pete's letter until I found what I was looking for. I pulled out a quarter and tossed it to him. The quarter caught the early morning light from the casement windows as it spun through the air. Bennie reached out one hand and snagged it, pulling it to him. He didn't say a word, just stared.

"We never finished our game," I said.

Bennie shrugged and tossed me the basketball. He made a little bowing motion as he stepped away from the basket.

I tried to remember what it felt like to shoot baskets, before I broke my arm, before I met Bennie, back when I loved to play for no other reason than to play. I lined up, flexed my knees, and launched the ball. It whooshed through the hoop with barely a whisper. "Hey," I exclaimed.

"That's how you shot when I first knew you," Bennie observed before he grabbed the ball, eyed the basket, and made the next shot. We played to five and then to ten.

"I wrote to my father on Sunday," Bennie said. "I asked him to send me money. I will take the train to Florida, where the carnival is working for the winter, and join him. What do I need with school?" His voice broke.

I blinked. It was what I had wanted all season, but now I shook my head. "You can't go," I said. "The team needs you." I crouched and eyed the basket. This was my favorite type of shot, from way outside. "You and George. In the front court. You'll take us all the way to the state tournament." I tossed the ball. It arched in the air, spinning perfectly.

189

I watched as it caught the rim and rocketed to the left, out of bounds.

"You win," I said, feeling slightly stunned. I took a deep breath. "Write to your father again. Tell him that you won. And tell him that you want to stay."

"And next year?" Bennie asked. He rebounded the ball and dribbled while he spoke.

"Next year, too."

I started to leave, but then stopped, pulled something from my pocket, and walked back to Bennie. "I . . . I want you to have this," I said.

He traced the stone with his fingers. "It's a basketball. Did you carve this?"

I nodded.

He studied me for a moment. "Thank you." He put the carving in his pocket, and then turned his attention back to the basket.

I left the gymnasium and walked to the newspaper office. Mrs. Pickens grabbed the camera and my story eagerly. "Father will develop the film," she said as she scanned my headline. "And I'm going to set this story into type myself. We'll run an extra edition. The newspapers from as far away as Indianapolis and Chicago are going to be interested in this." She nodded. "I'm impressed, Andy."

Gene Swango hollered at me as I was leaving. "Hey, Andy! Got something for your dad. Come and look." It was nearly time for school, but I changed direction and followed him to the mill. He led me out to the back where they kept gravel and extra stone. "You ain't going to be able to carry 'em."

"My arm's all better," I said. I waved it up and down. "Look."

He laughed, and then pointed. Half a dozen cylinders, the size of baseball bats only made out of stone, were stacked on the ground. I bent down to examine them. "Your dad's been after us to come out to your farm and drill some cores for the longest time," he said. "It ain't warm enough to be quarrying, but we were able to go out last week. Look what we pulled out. Some of 'em might be cracked from the cold, but your dad'll get the idea."

I rubbed the rock with my fingers. "Did this come from our quarry?" I asked. "The abandoned quarry?"

Gene grinned and nodded. "Ain't gonna be abandoned no more. Your granddaddy was just digging in the wrong spot. You got some prime limestone there, and a lot of it as near as I can tell. You tell your dad to get that stone out of the ground and throw it my way. My men'll carve it up so it'll build a palace."

"Limestone," I said. I rolled the word, with all its meanings, around on my tongue. "You mean, it's been there this whole time?"

"This whole time," he said. "Just under your feet, and you didn't even know it." He snapped his fingers. "There's a word for that, ain't there? Ira . . . iro . . . something?"

"Ironic," I said. Then I grinned. "From the Greek."

Chapter Thirty

The Pierre Carvers beat Franklin in our last regular game of the season. As we looked ahead to sectionals, my newspaper article, "Local Sheriff Caught!" exploded across the state. Felix left town the day before state officers arrived with a warrant for his arrest. Ham said he thought his uncle went to Chicago, but even he wasn't sure. Since Felix privately held Dad's mortgage, when he left, the mortgage went with him. Dad's face lost its haggard expression. He began construction on a large derrick near the site of the abandoned quarry. He planned to start pulling stones from the ground in May. Mother started playing bridge with Claudette Mortimer again, and George began to seriously consider some of the letters he had received from colleges.

Every evening after we finished chores and supper, George and I practiced basketball until late into the night. George knew all of Coach's plays and defenses down to the last detail, and with his meticulous help I learned back guard.

The team looked great. Everyone in town said so, and excitement crackled in the late winter air. We breezed through sectionals and then won our regional games by the largest margin in the school's history. "All Roads Lead to Indianapolis!" blared my headline in the *Journal*.

On the morning of the first round of the state tournament games, everyone in town who owned an automobile drove to Indianapolis. Those without automobiles met at the Pierre depot and boarded the train, which was making a special run to the capital. It was the farthest I'd ever been away from home.

Dad followed the convoy to the Indianapolis Coliseum. I'd never seen so many people together in one place. The Indiana State Fair grounds were filled with row after row of automobiles. Men in dark pants and white shirts escorted ladies wearing fancy dresses and hats. People thronged toward the Coliseum. The team and fans from Pierre moved toward the entrance. I approached the large limestone building with its three-tiered roof in awe. The Indianapolis newspaper said the tournament would host sixteen basketball teams and more than fifteen thousand fans.

A man in a three-piece suit approached me as I gazed at the building.

"My name's Ernie Howell, from Indiana University," he said. "Are you from the Pierre team?"

I nodded.

"I'm looking for a player by the name of Soaring."

"You want my brother, George," I said, pointing to where George stood with Hank and Stilt.

He shook his head. "No, I think it's you I want. You're Andrew Soaring? I've read some of your articles for the *Pierre Journal* and I'm impressed. When it's time for you to think about college, I hope you'll consider Indiana. We have a strong course of study in journalism."

I started to laugh, but then realized he was serious. I shook his hand. "Thank you, sir," I said. "But right now I just want to play basketball."

As the man walked away, Bennie approached me. He didn't say anything. We just stood together staring at the Coliseum. Bennie held the carving I'd given him and rolled it over and over in his hand.

"Bennie! Andy!" AnnaLise raced toward us through the milling crowd. "There must be thousands and thousands of people here!" The green bow in her short hair bobbed as she spoke.

We just nodded as players from other teams brushed past us.

"What are you doing? What is that?" AnnaLise grabbed Bennie's hand and looked at the carving. "Oh, wow. Another one! You should be a carver, Bennie. This is swell."

"I didn't make it. I can't carve." Bennie tilted his head toward me. "Andy gave it to me."

AnnaLise stared at me for a long moment. "You made this? And the horse? Did you make that, too?"

I nodded.

AnnaLise's eyes widened. Then she stomped her foot. "Oh! You boys! Why didn't you just say something?" she exclaimed before leaning over and kissing me on the cheek. She handed the basketball carving back to Bennie and raced into the crowd.

Ham muscled his way toward us. "Did my sister just *kiss* you?" He made a face. "Aww, Andy."

Bennie looked at me quizzically. "C'mon," I muttered. "Let's get inside."

We beat Anderson in the first round and North Manchester in the quarterfinal to match up against Martinsville in the semifinal game. If we beat them, we'd go to the championship. At halftime we were leading by two. Bennie was easily having his best game of the season, on course to break Pete's scoring record. I had scored two points and made three assists from my position at back guard.

"Keep doing what you're doing," Coach said after the break as he sent us back out onto the floor. "You've all learned a lot this year. Now I just want you to go out there and play basketball."

As I trotted out to the court, I glanced into the crowd. Mother and Dad were standing hand in hand, wearing their best church clothes and smiling, next to the Judge and Claudette Mortimer. Ham was whispering something to the boy next to him. The boy pulled a quarter from his pocket and fingered it, but then the Judge yanked the collar of Ham's shirt. I didn't look at AnnaLise. Thinking about her made my cheeks hot. I saw Mrs. Pickens sitting in the front row next to a group of reporters in three-piece suits. She wore a man's jacket over a light blue flapper dress. She was writing furiously.

"All right, Stilt!" I clapped as he prepared for the jump shot. The referee blew his whistle and held the ball between the two centers. The gymnasium hushed.

"Young man? Young man!" called a high-pitched voice. There was a gasp from the crowd. I turned to look. Mrs. Mortimer tottered across the court toward me. "Young man, can you help me? I'm . . . I'm lost. I can't find . . ." She patted my arms and then stared into my face. "Why, it's Peter Soaring! What are you doing here, Peter? It must be near time for you to leave for France."

I could feel the stares of the crowd, the referees, and the two teams. Mrs. Mortimer adjusted my jersey. "You look so dapper in your uniform," she said. She held my face between two bony hands. "You're a good boy, Petey. I know you must be scared. But you just remember that the whole town loves you, and that we're behind you all the way."

"Yes, ma'am," I whispered because she seemed to want me to say something.

"Granna!" Ham ran out onto the court. "Sorry," he said to the referee, who was approaching with a puzzled look on his face. "Come on, Granna. Time to go."

"I'm lost," Mrs. Mortimer said, directing her attention to Ham as he led her off the court. "Do you know where I live, young man? It's the stone house on the hill. . . ."

After she left, the referee again blew the whistle for the jump. I had a strange feeling in my chest as Stilt leaped into the air and tipped the ball toward me. I dribbled down the court and sent a fast pass to George. He passed to Bennie, who quickly scored.

We played the best basketball we had ever played as a team. The lead changed hands half a dozen times as both teams battled up and down the court. When the final whistle blew, I looked at the scoreboard.

Martinsville forty. Pierre thirty-eight.

My head dropped. We'd lost. All that work, all that effort, for nothing.

As we lined up to congratulate the Martinsville team, a roar of cheers erupted from the Pierre fans. I looked at the scoreboard again, wondering if I'd read it wrong. I hadn't. We had lost. But still the Pierre fans cheered.

"Good game," said the Martinsville player who'd shadowed me the entire game. He nodded toward the bleachers. "They sure think so."

Mother and Dad made their way through the crowd and down to the court. Dad reached out and pulled me and George close.

I sank into Dad's hug. I breathed in his smell of wool and shaving lather as I listened to the cheers. Over his shoulder I looked at the faces of the town. Everyone was there, everyone I cared about. Only Felix Mortimer was conspicuously absent.

I caught a glimpse of Mrs. Mortimer, waving and cheering with everyone else. Maybe she wasn't as crazy as everyone thought. I felt tears prick my eyes. She had known. Pete had kept his promise after all. He had come—come to cheer me on at the state tournament. And now I knew he had been with me all along.

Author's Note

Basketball has been a passion in Indiana since the game was introduced to the state in 1893. The popularity of Dr. James Naismith's recreational invention in Springfield, Massachusetts, grew throughout the country, but in Indiana, the fascination with the game exploded. The makeup of the state seemed ideal for the sport. Indiana was filled with small towns, with many of the schools too small to field an eleven-man football team. But they could always find five boys willing to play basketball. In addition, much of the state was involved with farming, with their busiest times in the spring, summer, and fall. Farm work was less intense during the winter months, so people had more time to follow their favorite sport.

Basketball became so important to Indiana that even Dr. Naismith noticed. "Basketball really had its beginning in Indiana, which remains today the center of the sport," he said in 1936 at a YMCA event in Indianapolis.

When Andy played, the game was a little different from how it's played today. There were no television time-outs and no electronic scoreboards. They didn't use a shot clock or a have a three-point shot. After every basket, both teams returned to the center for a jump ball, and until 1923 anyone on the team could shoot the free throw, regardless of who was fouled. But the essential elements remained the same—five (minimum) players on each team, battling offensively and defensively to shoot a basketball through a hoop and score two points.

In addition to high school and college teams, Sunday school

leagues, and YMCA groups, professional basketball also has a rich heritage in Indiana, one that dates back to 1913. There were no big-league NBA contracts early in the sport's history. Instead, players had regular jobs, and they played basketball, occasionally earning a little extra pocket money, for fun. Early teams included the Indianapolis Em-Roes and the Fort Wayne Caseys. Admission to the games ran anywhere from five cents for games against local teams to one dollar and fifty cents for the heralded match-up between the Celtics (New York) and the Caseys.

The first official state high school basketball tournament was played in 1911, with Crawfordsville High School taking top honors. Sectional play, before the state playoffs, began in 1915.

Pierre is a fictional team, and the basketball matchups presented in *Throwing Stones* are also fictionalized. The schools they played, however, all had basketball teams at that time. Martinsville did win the state championship in 1924 at the old Indianapolis Coliseum, but against Bedford in the semifinal game and Frankfort for the championship.

In April 1917, America entered World War I, and students became soldiers as many young men across the nation enlisted or were drafted. Approximately 117,000 men from the United States lost their lives in this War to End All Wars. But war wasn't the only thing claiming lives during this time. In 1918 and 1919, the Spanish Influenza became a worldwide pandemic, killing around 675,000 Americans both at home and abroad. Many schools were ordered closed until the epidemic subsided.

In January 1920, the eighteenth amendment to the United States Constitution, making it illegal to make, sell, or drink alcoholic beverages, went into effect. Indiana had already decided to "go dry" on July 1, 1919. The intention of Prohibition was to bring an end to the damaging effect that alcohol had on individuals, families, and society. But what it did, ultimately, was to push the manufacture, distribution, and consumption of alcohol underground, resulting in an increase in backwoods stills and bathtub gin, rumrunners, official bribery, and organized crime. The amendment was repealed in 1933.

The decade from 1920 to 1929 is often referred to as the Roaring Twenties. After the war, the economy boomed. Many people had money, and now they had more ways to spend their money. Automobiles, invented at the turn of the century, became less expensive and more popular. Many of the roads were gravel and dirt, and cars didn't have heaters, radios, or in most cases, windows, but automobile transportation became the wave of the future, with many families traveling away from their hometowns for the first time.

People, mostly in larger towns and cities, wired their homes for electricity. By the midtwenties, about half of Americans had electricity in their homes. Most of the electricity was used for lights, but modern conveniences such as vacuum cleaners, electric irons, and refrigerators began to hit the marketplace, fueled by the growth of a new industry—advertising.

Movies were a popular source of entertainment, but before 1927, all movies were silent. They were also all in black-and-white. The television had not yet been invented. Newspapers were the primary source of information, and towns both large and small depended upon the local paper for news and gossip.

Radio broadcasting began in 1920. At that time there were few radio receivers to pick up the broadcast, but the radio craze had begun. Between 1923 and 1930, some 60 percent of American families purchased a radio, which quickly became a source of news and entertainment. Crystal radios were among the first to be used and manufactured. Listeners used a piece of lead galena crystal and a cat whisker to find a radio signal. Edwin Armstrong worked to replace the crystal with a vacuum tube. Vacuum tube radios were introduced to the market in 1924.

Many of the country's farmers didn't experience the prosperity felt by the rest of the country. During the war, prices for grain and livestock skyrocketed as much of Europe had to import food from America. Farmers began to mortgage their land to buy new and more productive farming equipment. But after the war, prices plummeted. Many farmers couldn't sell their grain for enough money to buy the next year's seed. Times were tight for America's farmers even before the Great Depression, which started with the stock market crash on October 29, 1929.

Not all of Indiana was devoted to farming. In a small strip of southern Indiana, chiefly Lawrence and Monroe counties, much of the industry revolved around limestone. This area of the country contains the largest, most accessible outcropping of quality building stone in the world. The land is piled with boulders and dotted with gaping holes from which the stone was mined for many of the country's greatest buildings—the National Cathedral, the Pentagon, the Empire State Building, Rockefeller Center, a number of state capitals, and countless other structures. Regardless of where you live, chances are you will find a building, monument, or memorial made out of Indiana limestone. During the heyday of the limestone industry in the 1920s, nearly 70 percent of the cut stone in the United States came from this small strip of land.

The Rules of Basketball

❦❦❦

The original rules of basketball, which were written by Dr. James Naismith in 1892, have undergone quite a few changes over the years. The original rules read as follows:

1. The ball may be thrown in any direction with one or both hands.

2. The ball may be batted in any direction with one or both hands [never with the fist].

3. A player cannot run with the ball. The player must throw it from the spot on which he catches it, allowance to be made for a man who catches the ball when running if he tries to stop.

4. The ball must be held by the hands. The arms or body must not be used for holding it.

5. No shouldering, holding, pushing, tripping or striking in any way the person of an opponent shall be allowed; the first infringement of this rule by any player shall come as a foul, the second shall disqualify him until the next goal is made, or, if there was evident intent to injure the person, for the whole of the game, no substitute allowed.

6. A foul is striking at the ball with the fist, violation of Rules 3, 4, and such as described in Rule 5.

7. If either side makes three consecutive fouls, it shall count as a goal for the opponents (consecutive means without the opponents in the meantime making a foul).

8. A goal shall be made when the ball is thrown or batted from the grounds into the basket and stays there, providing those defending the goal do not touch or disturb the goal. If the ball rests on the edges, and the opponent moves the basket, it shall count as a goal.

9. When the ball goes out of bounds, it shall be thrown into the field of play by the person touching it. He has a right to hold it unmolested for five seconds. In case of a dispute the umpire shall throw it straight into the field. The thrower-in is allowed five seconds; if he holds it longer it shall go to the opponent. If any side persists in delaying the game the umpire shall call a foul on that side.

10. The umpire shall be the judge of the men and shall note the fouls and notify the referee when three consecutive fouls have been made. He shall have power to disqualify men according to Rule 5.

11. The Referee shall be judge of the ball and shall decide when the ball is in play, in bounds, to which side it belongs, and shall keep the time. He shall decide when a goal has been made and keep account of the goals, with any other duties that are usually performed by a referee.

12. The time shall be two fifteen-minute halves, with five minutes' rest between.

13. The side making the most goals in that time shall be declared the winner. In the case of a draw the game may, by agreement of the captains, be continued until another goal is made.*

Several significant rule changes were made in the years between 1892 and when Andy played in 1923:

1894	Free throw adopted as penalty for fouls.
1896	Five players on each team necessary for an "official" game.
1898	Dribbling the ball legalized.
1906	Open-end baskets legalized.
1908	Double dribble prohibited.
1910	Player with four fouls disqualified.
1912	Ten-second rule in backcourt adopted.

---

*James Naismith, *Original Basketball Rules*, 1892.